Copyright@2007 by Deborah Cardona

Déjà Vu Publications

All rights reserved, including the right of reproduction in whole
or in part in any form.

Printed in the United States of America

The Library of Congress has catalog ed the soft cover edition
as follows:

Cardona, Deborah

A Better Touch

ISBN Number

978-1-60402-278-0

Artwork By

Marion Designs

Edited By

A. V. Finigan-Hutchines

Dedicated to

Everyone in my life who believed in me

Acknowledgement

This book is dedicated to all of the women and men who are locked down in a NYS Correctional Facilities. You may be asking yourself why these individuals, well let's just say that I can relate. Giving shout outs to them is my way of saying hold your head and believe in dreams because dreams really do come true. The trick is figure out what you want and go for it. Now let me go on to thank the people who inspired me to write this book. First I would like to thank my higher power because of this divine energy I was able to get through one of the worse times in my life. I made it through with faith and patience and for that I will be eternally grateful. Secondly I would like to thank my best friend my mom Jane Padilla, mom we have seen some hard times in our lives, we have gotten through them together and sometimes apart .The main thing is that we got through them. Thank you for always being there for me I love you. The scarifies do not go unnoticed, my dad Albert Castro for giving me the gift of language the gift of writing you have passed on to me and my son will be valued forever. By expressing myself through words I was able to write not only one book but three. Thanks dad I love you. My step-dad Michael Padilla who I admire whole heartily you are a great man, father and husband Thank you for your unconditional love. My Step -mother who has always supported me through the good and bad time thanks. My four sons Marcus, David also none as D-monic CEO of Dirty Muzik Ent., Angel who I owe so much love to we will be together soon baby and Damion my little one mommy loves you, you guys are my true inspiration, and because of you I am a better woman. This book is for you hope you guys can grow up to be gentle lovely men. I am very proud to be your mother. My princess Déjà Marie my one and only baby girl. Grand mom is about to shine and as the foundation of this family I must maintain a strong and solid influence in your life. You will be the next president of this company so be ready to grow, learn and work (LOL). Now let's move on to the man who I truly feel began all of this my husband Harris Cardona. I found that because of you I am a stronger more independent woman you taught me to look beyond the pain we have endured and move on. Thank you for loving me the way that you do. My friends Patti, Rosie and China. No matter where I am in this world I will always remember the love and support you guys have given me Thank you all for choosing me. I say choosing because true friendship is an option not an obligation. Bebe you know that I can never forget my sweet little Diva hurry home we have a lot of work to do. Bruni my friend to the end we have seen the streets from another point of view and yet we survived. I love you, thank you for always being there. Remember I'm' the boss of you (LOL). Brenda Christian the author of "Til Death and Beyond" we are well on our way to success. Hold your head up because only the strong survive Thanks for all of your support. Freedom without you I could have never pulled it off Thanks for believing in me. China (Norma Martinez) you took the back seat for a long time thanks for giving me that space I needed to finish this book hope you enjoy the results of that. You mean the world to me.Last but never least my readers I hope you will enjoy this book and remember things are not always what they seem.

Love Is Love

Sexy

A Better Touch

Chapter 1

Six months and it was finally over. The graduating class had over 150 Correctional Officers who would now be assigned to the various Correctional Facilities located throughout New York State. Déjà accepted her certificate of completion, said her formal, "Thank You," then walked out before anyone noticed. She had no intentions of standing around and fronting. As she stepped out into the lobby, she could still hear the applause echoing throughout the hall.

As far as she was concerned these people were signing their lives away. Dedicating the next 25 years to the prison system, "How stupid could they be," is what she thought as she continued to walk quickly towards the exit doors .Déjà had other plans and there was no time like the present to begin her journey. Déjà is 25 years old, and becoming a C.O. at a women's correctional facility was just part of what she had in mind. Phase one was completed. Phase two was becoming one of the biggest Ma'dams this side of the globe .With two kids and a whole lot of dreams; she was convinced that she had to do much more than the average chick. She was going to become the ultimate Lady. Déjà had come a long way from having bruised faces and broken ribs and now was her time to shine.

She married her High School sweetheart, upon graduating high school, who turned out to be abusive - at first verbally, then physically. All the love in the world wouldn't allow her to live a life of one ass whipping after the other. So after years of abuse, Déjà left with the clothes on her back. The only packages she carried along with her were the ones she had brought into this world, her daughters. With no family and very few friends, thanks to her so called husband, Déjà had no place to go. She found herself standing in front of the 23rd Precinct where a domestic violence unit was located.

After several hours of intense questioning, Déjà and her girls were placed in a domestic violence shelter where she began to piece her life back together again. At first she wasn't sure if this is where she wanted to be, however there wasn't any doubt in her mind that this is where she needed to be in order to recover from all the drama she had endured.

Déjà couldn't continue to live her life in fear, so her wants and needs had to be put on hold at that point. Reflections of her bounced off the mirrors that surrounded the main lobby of the State Capital Building, dressed in a simple low-cut black strapless dress By Dolce & Gabbana, black 3"inch patent leather thong sandals by Gucci, and to make the outfit complete she wore a black veil designed by Vera Wang's Wedding Collection. She looked as though she was attending a funeral and not the ceremony of a new career. In many ways this is the effect she wanted to capture; burying the past along with the memories, her outfit represented exactly that - a life of darkness and pain. It was o.k. for today though because starting tomorrow she had plans of transforming herself into a ghetto-fied bitch.

There would be no more confessions of the soul for Déjà; no more late night talks with Mrs. Negron, her domestic Violence Counselor. Although she had to admit that she would miss those talks because Mrs. Negron had been there to help her heal from the inside, never once judging her for whom she was or wasn't.

"Ms. Padilla, you can come in now," Mrs. Negron called out as she motioned Déjà into her office. "You may take a seat by my desk or you may want to sit over by the waterfall, believe me the sound of the water falling amongst the stones can bring a comforting feeling. It can also work wonders on your soul." Mrs. Negron's smile was enough to light up the room.

Teresa Negron was a strong believer in nature, so in order to get one of her clients to relax and share their experience with her; she had to provide them a comfortable environment. Generally it worked, making her position as a Social Worker all the more successful. Déjà had decided to sit by the waterfall after several minutes of looking around the office. It was no bigger than a salad bowl but what it represented was something much more magical than that - the colors and sounds projected peace and tranquility, something Déjà was desperately searching for. Never had she experienced anything so peaceful. For years her life had become one battle after another, not to mention that she had always felt so out of place in her world. But not in this room; in this room she became aware of her inner being, learning that this world wasn't hers alone and that what her husband did to her was not her fault. In this room she began to find herself.

In the beginning, Déjà had found the woman to be a little strange, and then she had become fascinated by her. From the moment she entered Mrs. Negron's office she could feel the aura of peace surrounding her. It was kind of creepy now that she thought about it. The office just didn't belong inside of the old structured building. When Déjà had first arrived at Our Lady of Hope, she was welcomed by a group of women who were like her - survivors.

The welcoming committee sang song, held up signs, hugged and embraced her as though she was a runaway child who was found by the local police and brought back home. Déjà didn't want to be rude by saying what she really felt, so she just went along for the ride in hopes of getting out of there as soon as possible. In all reality she had found all that drama corny as hell because it cramped her style. All she needed was a place where she could get her thoughts together; a place where her children would be safe.

If it weren't for the kids, Déjà would have walked away from her sorry ass husband a long time ago. This was her only way out, so she wasn't there to make friends. Now 12 months later all the visible scars had been healed. The emotional scares were the ones with the most damage though, the ones that needed a serious makeover. Déjà couldn't seem to break through her mental function; how she thought and what she thought of had remained the same. Nothing was going to stand in her way of doing what she needed to do. She now held the master key to make all of her dreams come true.

Her feelings about her peers had not changed either. They came across as being needy because these women never made the effort, nor took the steps necessary to change their circumstances. These women were afraid of moving on, so they clung to the security of the shelter, never having the opportunity to exhale. Déjà didn't feel as though she was better than them - JUST DIFFERENT!

Déjà was not about to do the same. Taking the corrections test and passing at the top of her class was the first step to changing her circumstances. Although in the beginning it was thought of as a way into independence, it was now a way of getting even. No man would be safe! Any man who came into her circumference would be drained of all monies and property. But worse of all they would lose their dignity because the power behind the pussy was a dangerous thing. Anything outside of that was irrelevant. This is what she planned to instill in the young ladies that she would recruit. They would be the best group of lady soldiers the ghetto had to offer. Her ladies would have style, class, and grace among other things. Most importantly they will be loyal to the force driven behind the cause. They would be ride and die bitches - true thug-ettes.

She smiled at the thought. The applause was slowly dying down. That was a sure sign that the ceremony was coming to an end. Déjà turned away from the mirrors that surrounded her and then headed towards the exit doors. Behind those doors

13

was a whole new life awaiting Ms. Déjà Padilla and she couldn't wait to get started. First she had to go pick up Nadiva and Breanne and their belongings from the shelter. Then they would all be headed to Albion N.Y. with a dollar and a dream. Déjà ran out of the building, inhaled some fresh air, and then hailed a cab. "Where to Ms.," the cab driver asked as he flipped on the meter. "To prison if I don't pray or to the bank if I do." Her laughter could be heard from blocks away as the cabbie pulled away from the curb.

Chapter 2

Her first day at work and already she was late, five minutes to be exact. Getting her daughters ready for school had taken her longer then she had intended. Rushing through the front gates of Albion Correctional Facility, she noticed several other officers standing in line waiting to be assigned to their post for the day. Roll call and count time were her most important tasks.

She rushed and took her place in line. Out of breath she answered the Sergeant when he called out her name "Here sir," Déjà proclaimed her attendance with a confident tone. She was ready for her first day at Albion. "You will be working on housing unit J-2," the sergeant ordered while looking down at his clipboard, then back at her. Déjà nodded her head up and down in a yes motion. There was no need to verbally respond because she understood perfectly what it was that she needed to do.

This job was just the stepping stone for the bigger job that lay ahead, so she held onto her intent silently. Déjà grabbed her knapsack filled with odds and ends, things that she would need throughout the day. There were a few little extras for the ladies she would eventually select for her pussy pound. Déjà was a natural at seduction, with her Carmel skin, long curvy black hair, and hazel eyes, a gift from her grandmother, had been caused most to become mesmerized by her beauty. Something she most definitely had to use to draw in some of the most attractive girls walking the compound. Déjà had to seduce them

15

into believing that she was their only sense of security. In an environment such as prison it would be easy to do.

Many women were without the basic necessities such as soap, shampoo & deodorant, and being able to smoke a Newport was another issue all together. Déjà had plans to take care of those needs in exchange for their mind, bodies and eventually their souls. Déjà jumped into the blue van along with the other officers, as they rode down the path that lead to the back buildings. She thought about how many times she had to come close to being a statistic like the ladies that now roamed the walkways.

Déjà was no different from any of the women here; she was just one of the lucky ones because she had found enough courage to walk away from all the madness that had surrounded her life. With all of the chaos now behind her she walked into her assigned block with only one mission in mind.

"Good morning ladies," Déjà said to the ladies who sat in the rec-area drinking their morning coffee, reading newspapers or playing cards. Some responded while others looked at her like she was crazy. They weren't use to the officers at Albion showing any signs of concern. Good morning, good afternoon, nor good evening were words that were limited throughout the jail between staff and inmate. There were a certain degree of recognitions between the two. The rules and regulations given to her by her superiors went against everything she had planned to do. Déjà had decided way before she started the job that she would be that one C.O. who would do what she

16

wanted when she wanted. Déjà was on the prowl for some live stock and she was going to make it her business to find it.

First she relieved the 11pm to 7am officer, and then took her place on the throne. Inmates walked passed her, glancing in her direction, whispering amongst each other asking who the new kid on the block were. She glanced back at them with a kool-aid smile. "Good morning ladies." Again some acknowledged her, and some didn't. They were too busy trying to get their gossip on early in the morning. Some walked right by her rubbing the sleep out of their eye while their private parts giggled.

Titties and ass were everywhere, just the way Déjà liked it. She had definitely died and gone to pussy heaven. Because of what she had in mind this was the perfect place to be. Here she could hand pick the ladies that she wanted to work her stable. The pimp game had become one of violence and betrayal by both pimps and whores, but her ladies of the night wouldn't be any of the two they would be beautiful, intelligent, sexy, soft, and filled with sexual energy and violence did not fit into the equation. Getting paid among other things, like getting a decent education, were the only things she needed for her ladies to have in mind. The ladies needed to be hungry for the finer things in life, even if it meant selling their goods to feed their appetite. If for any strange reason any one of them lacked in one area, Déjà was willing to teach and guide them towards perfection. It wouldn't cost her a thing to sacrifice her time because it would be worth it at the end.

Investing in this type of project would be beneficial to her a well as the ladies. Right now her main concern was appearing unexpectedly to those she thought had potential. She would worry about their imperfections at another time. First she had to pick from the harvest that grew daily. The prison system was like a revolving door; when one person left, five others would enter and sometimes one person would return often on violations, if not on a violation they would return with a new number. Her girls were promised to never return as long as they followed her instructions. Their lives would be changed forever, guaranteed. Slowly, but surely, she would achieve that goal. No one would be able to stop the unstoppable.

Déjà had been in such a deep trance thinking about the future and all that had to be done, when she realized that all sixty women who lived on J-2 stood before her. "Hey officer what's your name?" "Excuse me" Déjà stated as she finally realized that she was being talked to. "What's your name? I know you don't want me or the others to call you officer all day ". One of the inmates asked with base in her voice. "No of course not. My name is Padilla." "What's your name"? Déjà threw back with even more attitude.

"Jheri (Jah-we) Wright stated, in her West Indian accent as she walked off. "Hey Jheri wait up. How you just going to walk away like that. What's the attitude all about," Déjà questioned as she followed her outside the dorm and into the rec-area. "Ain't none, I just don't fuck with police like that." "I hear you. But let me let you know, right now, that I'm no ordinary C.O." Déjà's smirk made Jheri feel uneasy. "What do you mean by that?" "I'm not going to answer that right now you'll see how I am as time goes on." Déjà took a pack of Newport 100's out of her pocket, and then asked, "You smoke?" "Yeah I smoke."

Déjà took one cigarette out of the pack then walked out onto the front porch. When she noticed that Jheri had not followed her, she jerked her head in a come here motion. Déjà lit her cigarette, took a long drag, and then passed Brooklyn the rest of the pack. "What's this for," Jheri questioned while lighting a cigarette of her own. "It's an investment." "Oh yeah what kind of investment," Jheri had to question her last statement.

Jheri's mind went on overdrive. Why? Because Jheri was gay and she had already noticed Déjà's intoxicating aura, her eyes and her soft full lips, something she wouldn't mind having wrapped around her clit. Her sex appeal said come fuck me all day long. Even in her blue uniform she was saying something appealing, so imagine what she looked like in street clothes.

"Well baby boy let me begin by saying that I have some major plans and I have chosen you to help me out". "Oh yeah what makes you so sure I'm a go along with anything you have to offer"? Now moving in closer, she wanted to hear what Ms. Padilla had to say. Her curiosity had gotten the best of her. "Oh I'm sure, baby. Believe me; I'm going to make it worth your while."

Déjà could definitely work with her. Besides, who better to pull in the ladies then a bona-fide dyke, one that would capture the ladies' attention by her manly presence with her coco complexion, soft sexy bedroom eyes and amazingly strong physique, Jheri was sure to have the women at Albion leaking all over themselves.

It had surprised Déjà to view Jheri in that manner. She wasn't gay and has never found anyone of the same sex appealing, however like everything else in this world there was a first time for everything. Finding someone attractive, especially someone who held the same equipment was nothing more than just giving them the hands up on their appearance. Déjà brushed the thought out of her mind then went back into the unit, leaving Jheri with something to think about. In time all will be revealed.

Chapter 3

From a woman's point of view pimping can become an extremely difficult job. Twenty four hours a day one had to submit themselves to the lifestyle. Selling ass, especially someone else's was definitely not a job for someone who thought small. Déjà was going to run her house like a big corporation. Sort of like Nestles, the only difference between the two would be where Nestles sold chocolate; Déjà would have a variety of candy. There is nothing like going into a candy store and purchasing the type of goodies your taste buds craved. Strawberry, cherry, coco, and even vanilla will be on standby for the picking.

However before she was able to open up the shop they had to find a place big enough where her clientele could call a place of their own, even if for a short time. It would be theirs, a place where all of their fantasies could come true without the interferences of the outside world; a pleasure retreat, somewhere private where they can find physical pleasures without any of the commitments, for the right price that is. Déjà arrived at the real estate office for her first appointment with Mr. Dunn, a short middle aged man with a receding hair line.

Before she entered the office, which was located at his private home, she reached into her purse to retrieve a brochure she had come across at one of the local stores. Her thoughts went back to her brief conversation with him. "Dunn realtors, how can I help you?" "Hello my name is Déjà and I am looking for a four bedroom home?" "Déjà, as in déjà vu?" "Yes." "And your last name ma'am?" Déjà had never once thought about *not* using her real last name. Thinking about it now she believed it would be wise to use an a.k.a. especially in this particular business venture. After reading several autobiographies written by professional Ma'dam's, Déjà decided to follow their advice and never use her government name to indulge in illegal activities.

"That is my last name sir, Vu." Déjà smiled a devious smile as she held the phone close to her ear. "Well Ms.Vu, I have an opening for 4pm. Will that be convenient for you?" "As a matter face that will be perfect." "O.k. I will see you then." Déjà slowly came out of her trance then rang the doorbell. She had already thought about the type of house she was looking for. It would have to be in a good location, discreet and spacey because if she was going to have more than one working girl she needed the space to accommodate them. As long as her ladies where comfortable in their surroundings, their performance was sure to be up to par.

Déjà waited patiently, while looking around in search of someone who would resemble the agent on the cover of the brochure. After several minutes of standing in the scorching sun, Déjà decided to walk around to the other side of the house. She noticed that there was at least two acres of green freshly cut grass, with two oak trees standing squarely in the middle of the backyard. The trees, which seemed to be there forever, gave the property a cozy atmosphere. The house that

22

was built on the land looked ancient, but yet well maintained. It was two stories high with a veranda circling the second floor.

The house was in a good location, just five minutes off the main road and yet it seemed like a million miles away. Déjà could envision her daughters running around as they played games, jumping rope and swinging from one of the trees. This was a place where she could raise her daughters. She wanted nothing more than to get them away from the grimy streets of New York City. Thankfully, she had awakened from the insults and abuse their father had placed upon her. Now she had the chance to give her daughters a healthy, normal life. Déjà heard footsteps coming slowly in her direction and before she was able to turn around she heard the voice she was already familiar with.

"Ms.Vu?" "Yes, Mr. Dunn," Déjà inquired as she held her hand out to shake his. "I became worried when you hadn't arrived for your four o'clock appointment. Then I noticed your car sitting in the driveway, but there was no sign of you, so I'd figured I'd find you out back … its charming isn't it," Mr. Dunn asked her while pointing out onto his property. "Yes it is extremely charming." "Would you be interested in something like this?" "Yes, one day." Déjà stated as she continued to look around. "Why don't we go inside so you can tell me what it is your looking for. I have several photos." Mr. Dunn continued with his sales pitch as he escorted Déjà into the house.

Once inside of the tiny room, Mr. Dunn used as an office, Déjà sat quietly on a leather chair. While the real estate agent

23

gathered some forms from a filing cabinet, she looked around the office and noticed several framed photos of family and friends sitting on the shelves, she also observed his desk which held frames too. However, with their backs facing her she was unable to view its contents. Curiosity controlled her next move. Not sure how Mr. Dunn would react she chanced it anyway. Déjà reached out and turned one of the larger frames in her direction. In the photo were four people, two adults and two small children, one girl, one boy and of course Mr. Dunn. She could tell by his appearance that the photo was taken during his younger years.

The woman who stood beside him in a loving way was sure to be his wife, if in fact the woman in the photo was the Mrs. She was attractive with a honey blond page boy, fair complexion and hazel chest-nut eyes. Her smile was an extreme sign of happiness. Déjà tried to think back to when there was a time in her life that she had taken a photo like this with her family. It saddened her that no image came to mind. On the same token it made her question what true happiness was really like.

Mr. Dunn had been standing, closely watching Déjà as she looked at the photo while running her freshly manicured nails softly on the outside frame. The way that she stroked the wooden piece enticed him. She moved her fingers, hands and wrist like a professional jewelry maker. He wouldn't mind getting his gold bar stroked by those beautiful hands. Mr. Dunn thought to himself as he lowered the file he had made for her in hopes of hiding his erection that now pushed up against his pants. He didn't want to intrude on her thoughts; nevertheless he thought it would be best to move forward with the business at hand.

"Ms. Vu." Mr. Dunn spoke gently as he took his place at his desk. "You seem intrigued by my family's photo." "Oh yes, I apologize for that," Déjà excused herself then placed the photo back. "No apology needed. That's an old photograph of me and my family. The kids are all grown up and in college, and the Mrs., well that's been over for a long time," Mr. Dunn stated as he sat back in his leather chair. He placed his hands over the bulge that now grew two extra inches.

Déjà noticed his moves and found it interesting that she had the power to make him feel the way that he did. Her awareness was developing pretty quickly since her decision to pursue a career in prostitution. Although she had never actually sold herself, she knew that one day she would have to. It would be part of the job. How could she convince other women to solicit and accept payment for sex if she had never experienced it herself? There was no time like the present, to dive in and get her pussy wet. "So, Mr. Dunn excuse me if I seem a little out of touch this is the first home that I plan to rent. I'm a little nervous." Déjà looked straight into her soon to be client's eyes while slightly opening her legs to expose tight but smooth thighs.

Before her arrival she had stopped by her place to change out of her uniform. She had chosen her attire with care, giving off a sophisticated but very sexy look. Déjà brushed her hand across

25

her black two piece Ann Taylor Suit, as if she were smoothing out the wrinkles.

However that was far from the truth. What she was doing was brushing pass the wrinkles while slowly bringing her skirt up a little higher. The shorter it became the more flesh was exposed for Mr. Dunn's pleasure. Saliva began to form on Dunn's tongue as his eyes roamed down the frame of her hour glass figure was just what he needed; because his wife had been so dead set on finding herself, she left their home leaving Dunn to resort to the occasional one night stands with different women.

Ciara Dunn had filed for divorce once the kids had gone off to begin their own lives because she felt trapped in a marriage that wasn't going anywhere. At least that is what she had expressed to the therapist Dunn had spent thousands of dollars on. She could have saved them a whole lot of money and time if she had only stood up for what she longed for many years ago, she blamed it on him, he blamed it on menopause, she blamed it on anything that would come to mind. However his stamina was strong, sometimes out beating the younger generation of women he had come into contact with. He was yet to meet one who could out last him in the bedroom.

"Ms. Vu, there is no need to be nervous you are in good hands." "I'm sure but renting a new home can be risky especially when you don't have a man to look over the structure of the house. Some things are not always what they seem," Déjà stated as she bit her bottom lip.

26

Becoming more confident in her quest Déjà realized that she was enjoying herself. The power, the control that she felt lead her to believe that she was about to make a great career move. "Yes I can agree with you on that," Mr. Dunn said softly in his baritone voice. "I can assume Ms. Vu that everything you're looking for is right here."

At this point the conversation was taking on a new twist, just the way Déjà wanted it to. "Mr. Dunn can I be honest with you." "Yes of course, but please call me Mike, Dunn is so formal." "Okay Mike. I am just a city girl who is in search of a better life and hopefully expand my business." "Oh and what business is that," Mike Dunn questioned as he shifted uncomfortably in his seat.

"Well I'm in the business of fulfilling fantasies." Déjà paused then continued slowly, "for a price that is." "Well Ms. Vu or can I call you Déjà?" "Déjà is fine." "I am also in the business of purchasing services for a price." Dunn was open. He knew exactly what Déjà was talking about and he definitely would pay the price because he liked what he saw sitting in front of him.

"Mike, I can see that you are a man about your business." Déjà smiled as she looked directly at Dunn's crotch. "You would be making a very good investment." Déjà now stood up then began to move towards him. "And you my dear have just been bought. Now remove all of those extra garments and show me what you got under there."

27

Chapter 4

Although it had been Déjà's first time exchanging her goods for funds, it was not as bad as she thought it would be. Basically Déjà just did what was asked of her. She had removed all of her clothing slowly, sort of like a stripper dancing to her favorite song. Little by little each piece fell to the floor around Mike's feet, while all along swaying her hips back and forth. The moves created extra moisture between her thighs something she thought was not possible. She imagined herself getting ready to fuck the man of her dreams, making the business proposition a whole lot easier to deal with.

Mike only wanted to fuck Déjà straight up; he didn't want anything extra like a blow job or anything, so it was pretty simple. Déjà danced her way onto Mike's lap from behind giving him a full view of her full round ass as she gently lowered herself onto his 8"inch muscle while gliding her hips in a sliding motion. The power, authority, and the force she had allowed herself to feel, as she took her first customer into another world, was beyond anything she had ever experienced while making love to her first love. But this wasn't love this was business.

After giving Mike Dunn what he had paid for, Déjà quickly grabbed her clothes then headed to the bathroom to wash up. She looked into the mirror applied a fresh coat of lip gloss then counted her money. Two hundred dollars is what she charged for the quickie she had just performed. Dunn didn't even last ten minutes once Déjà began to stroke his manhood with her walls. She pulled out a black organizer from her handbag then entered Dunn's name and number; she'd hope to one day fill the book to its full capacity with customers' names and a little extra data on what the gentlemen were into.

Déjà placed the book back into her purse along with her money then she exited the bathroom as though nothing had ever happened. Now she was ready to resume with her meeting. "So Mike are you ready to show me some of those properties?"

After taking a few laps around the yard Jheri had decided to sit down on one of the many wooden benches that surrounded her, she had sent her friend, Nick, a kite requesting her presence. As she waited for her friend's arrival, she remained in deep thought observing her surroundings like never before. Yeah, she always got her look on, but now things were different because she now had to recruit the women. Getting women to respond to her was second nature, but this would be different. Her skills will definitely be put to the test.

The yard at Albion Correctional Facility has always been an open market for the random chick. The institution was filled with robbers, hoodlums, drunks, addicts, street fighters, and street walkers. Sure these types of women would be an easy target, but what man would pay hundreds of dollars for ass he could possibly get for twenty and sometimes even less. Jheri had to find women with integrity, who would have class about what they did behind closed doors; nothing like the common

30

street hoe. What exactly would she be looking for? She hadn't a clue, but she would know once she saw it.

Déjà had told her that she needed at least six girls. One by one they would hopefully be released to a halfway house which Déjà would use as a front because it would actually be a pay to play parlor during the evening hours. The days would be used to further educate the minds of her ladies. The girls who worked for her had to obey first and foremost house rules, which she would later put into play. Most importantly the women will have to be ambitious, wanting more than just to lie on their backs. Déjà continued on, ending their brief conversation with, "The more they wanted out of life the more money they will make, making me the number one ma'dam in New York State."

At first Jheri thought that Déjà was a little off. Her mind changed quickly as Déjà described the benefits of her plan, making Jheri's appetite grow. Unexpectedly Natalie Dudley a.k.a Renee came into view. From across the yard Jheri watched Renee with different eyes. She glided across the manicured lawn in her tight fitting state issued greens and tiny V-neck t-shirt. Through her clothes Jheri could tell that Renee had an hour-glass figure, firm breasts tight thighs and an ass so fat a nigga could rest his head on it all day long. Her honey caramel complexion glowed making the moles on her face an added attraction. That's not even talking about her shoulder length hair that bounced with each step. In her cat like walk, Renee began to glide in Jheri's direction.

31

It had never been a secret how Renee felt about Jheri. Since day one Renee had wanted to swing an episode with her. She constantly fantasized about the things she would do to her, but never had the opportunity. Saliva seeped out of Jheri's mouth because she too daydreamed of stroking Renee deeply. She imagined Renee bent over at the waist as she dug deep inside of her causing her to speak out in tongues.

A slick smile appeared on Jheri's face as Renee got closer. "What's up Papa, What's good?" "Ain't nothing new what's up with you?" "You know, same old shit different day," Renee stated while looking straight into Jheri's deep set eyes. "Who you out here with, mind if I sit down." Renee quickly placed her firm ass on the bench before Jheri could say no.

"Nah I don't mind. I'm waiting on my man, got some politicking to do."

"I hear that." Renee found it unusual that Jheri was being pleasant towards her.

Although Jheri was well known for her hardcore brutal ways, which never stopped Renee from showing her interest. She found Jheri challenging. Natalie Dudley had never had a problem with attracting attention. She was beyond pretty and her conversation was up to par. She was a con woman, a professional credit card expert. Running up in someone's bank and coming out with thousands of dollars of someone else's money took finesse. The attraction that she brought forth was hypnotizing. Jheri however didn't give her the time of day, making Renee all the more intrigued. "Damn girl you looking good, working out or something?" "Papa you know that I work out on a regular." "I never noticed."

Jheri figured she'll play a little cat and mouse game with her and see how far it would go. Renee's face became serious. Jheri could sense that Renee didn't appreciate that response because her body language told it all. Jheri parlayed for a second then lit a cigarette; she took the first drag then passed it over to Renee. "I don't smoke Jheri." Renee now pouting turned her face away from her. "Oh now it's Jheri. What happened to calling me papa?" "I don't think you deserve the title. Sweet nothings are earned and you haven't put up." "Oh word, it's like that." "Yeah it is. I'll check you out later Jheri. Maybe one day when you learn to have a little more respect we'll talk."

Renee stood up abruptly then walked away, heading towards a group of women sitting close by at another table. Jheri couldn't believe just how fast she had fucked up that little encounter. Suddenly realizing that if she was to be part of Déjà's plan, she had better learn some social skills, and she better learn them fast. Pimping was totally different than what Déjà had in mind. Pimps were known to be aggressive, demanding that their women work hard long hours, under severe weather conditions and under strict rules. So the business ended up being a devastating experience that most women would eventually become tired of. It didn't matter one way or the other how the ladies would feel; pussy was on demand twenty four hours a day and they were expected to provide that pussy with no questions asked.

Street walkers who were ruled by an iron fist, never really reaping the benefits of the long hours they had put in. Yeah, they were sheltered and clothed, but occasionally even that was denied if they didn't meet their quota. Honest classy hard working hookers were hard to find now a days. Street hookers were considered to be hardened, cold hearted creatures with hollow souls.

Meanwhile, Renee stood by glancing from time to time in Jheri's direction. She wondered what Jheri had gone through in her life to make her bitter. Maybe one day she would ask her. "What's up girl what you thinking about," Destiny one of Renee's closet friends asked her. "I'm thinking about that fine ass nigga over there." "Who Jheri?" "Yeah can you believe he tried to break fly on me." "Yeah I can believe it; her conceited ass thinks it's all about her. That's why she can never get with a bitch like you."

Destiny had come from a long line of card players, a trade that was handed down through generations. Her grandmother and mother were both con artists. When Destiny had become old enough to talk a vic out of their pockets, she had received the gift of game. This is how she met Renee. Five years prior to their incarceration, Destiny had gone down to midtown. Since it was too late in the evening to hit the banks, she had to decided to go for the next best thing, jostling. It just so happened that Renee was out there doing the same exact thing; both standing on different sides of the street, both dressed in the finest wear and both out for the same thing.

Their vic walked slowly up 8th Avenue towards 43rd Street. They both observed the victims swagger. His arrogances was as though he was untouchable. As one began to cross the street to walk along side of him the other began to cross from the other direction. They both approached the gentleman in their no nonsense demeanor making eye contact, realizing that they were both out for the same thing.

Destiny had made the choice at that moment to fall back some, allowing Renee to proceed in the game of making a rough contact with the vic then slowly reaching for his wallet. Renee was halfway across the avenue when suddenly the gentleman began to scream, then began to run in her direction. "Stop that lady she just stole my wallet!" A look of panic came across Renee's face; however she was trained in transformation.

Meanwhile she tried to stay calm. Mr. Attitude grabbed Renee by the sleeve of her coat and spun her around. Destiny looked on at first with a good for your ass attitude, but then thought twice about hating on the player. Under the circumstances she wouldn't have looked back, however there was something about the way the vic grabbed her that got under her skin. If it would have been her standing there caught and ready to go to jail, she would have wanted someone to help her out. Destiny quickly decided to do just that. She crossed back over towards the couple. She stood directly in front of the vic and began to scream in his face, poking her index finger into his chest.

"I knew it. I knew your no good ass was cheating on me. So this is the bitch you have been spending all of your time with!" "What," the vic yelled in shock. "Who are you?" "Oh now you don't know who the fuck I am, you bastard." Renee began to struggle against the vic's grip as the strange woman who stood before them continued to fuss at him. She couldn't get over how luck had come out of nowhere, but she was very much aware that the other player was helping her out. So she took full advantage of the opportunity. Renee back slapped the vic across the face, than began her role as the mistress gone astray by his lies. "How dare you not tell me that you were married? What, you thought that I would never find out!"

Renee was finally able to release his grip. As soon as the other pedestrians noticed what was going on and began to stare at Renee, she gave Destiny the eye. The vic was to overwhelmed with embarrassment that he hadn't noticed that this was all a set up. As the ladies ran off with his wallet he couldn't do anything but just stand there. That day was the beginning of Renee and Destiny's friendship and the beginning of a different type of partnership.

"Come on girl let's take a walk," Destiny suggested as she pulled Renee away. "By the way have you noticed how good that nigga Nick has been looking lately?" "Yeah, there she goes right there," Renee said as she pointed in Nick's direction. Together they turned their heads to find Nick walking across the yard.

Chapter 5

Nick had been known around the facility as a ladies' man. Although she had been confronted by negativity which had led her to catch an assault charge, she still held the respectability of a charmer. Nick was attractive with baby soft coco skin, oval shaped eyes, and thick full lips that only spit pleasing and enchanting words. Her physique was tight in all areas, but her mental is what caused her to penetrate deep into the lady of the hour. To vibe with her, her seeker would have to have a lot of these same qualities. This is one of the reasons Nick was riding her bid out solo. She had yet to meet a woman who could flow on her level. Besides half the women in prison were trifling street level thug-ettes; some things she just couldn't flow with.

Five years into her sentence and she still hadn't met anyone who could capture her attention. Nick held her independence and need, was not part of her character, making Nick was the number one sort out she/he on the compound. She knew it and was flattered, but she was not interested. Jheri and Nick had met during one of Jheri's episodes. The Scenario: Jheri had a nice looking girl by the name of Coco who at times she caught drooling over Nick whenever she passed by.

Jheri had never been insecure about the competition; it was merely disrespectful on Coco's part to flirt with Nick while being with her. Naturally the short glances and lip licking motions Coco made planted a seed in Jheri head. She had decided that

Coco was going to respect her, regardless of what she thought. So as soon as Nick came into view, Jheri smacked the shit out of Coco knocking her sorry hoe-ish ass to the ground. What she hadn't planned on was for Nick to confront her on the situation.

Nick simply told Jheri that if a chick was going astray right before her eyes, then she had to take a look at how she was treating her to make her want to roam. She blessed Jheri with some positive jewels which eventually she would have to put into play, and there was no time like the present. When Déjà approached her and described what she needed, the first person she thought about was Nick. Nick was capable of making women come out of their panties without so much as a touch. Her words were lethal.

Nick had received Jheri's kite earlier in the day and wondered what was so important. She asked around if Jheri was cool and those who ran into her throughout the day said, "yeah." Jheri knew that Nick didn't play the yard like that because there was nothing out there to hold her interest. Nevertheless, she headed out to meet her. From a distance she noticed Renee and Destiny staring. Nothing new, Nick was used to the attention. There was something different in Renee's look that made Nick stare back. Maybe it was the glow on her face or maybe it was the way her greens fit like a pair of Seven Jeans. Whatever it was, Nick sure as hell liked what she saw.

Jheri stood seated as she watched the connection between Nick and Renee, jealousy creped up and of course suspicion.

Jheri shook the feeling, thinking that maybe she was overreacting; it was all sweet though because they were different in their own way. "Yo Nick," Jheri hollered, "I'm over here!" "I see you nigga!" Nick hollered back as she made a full complete turn while still staring at Renee. "Come on nigga. I got something important I need to talk to you about." "Alright then get your ass up and let's take a walk."

Nick was already heading towards the same track Renee was walking on. The swing in her hips was like a magnet, so Nick wanted to get a closer look. Jheri caught up with Nick just before she made her first round. "What's up with you? What the fuck is your rush?" "Ain't nothing I just wanted to take a walk. So what's so important," Nick asked while still looking at Renee's ass jiggle. "I have a business proposition for you." "Oh yeah." "Yeah listen I met this new C.O., who started working here today, and she put me on to some serious shit." "What," Nick asked while still looking straight ahead. "Why don't you just sit down so I can tell you?"

Jheri walked over to the bleachers that faced the baseball field and together they took a seat. Nick sat quietly, waiting for Jheri to continue; it was hard to believe that a C.O., especially a new one, would share anything with her or any other inmate for that matter. Although, it did happen from time to time, it was rare. Nick wasn't really into getting caught up in any jail house schemes but the curiosity was still there.

"Alright," Jheri began. "This morning I met a Ms. Padilla who came up here with some money making attitude. Yo, the bitch is bad Son! But that's beside the point. The point is that she is a Ma'dam and she is looking to recruit some of the women from here." "Why would she want to do that," Nick paused to think, then continued. "If in fact this so called Ma'dam is legit. Why would she want to deal with these women?" Nick now pointed at the variety before them.

"Because half of these women don't have a place to go once they get released. Most of them are going to end up in a halfway house. You know that 85% of the women in population go to half-way houses or shelters when they are released from here." "Then what?" "She told me was that she was going to use a half-way house as a front."

"Come on man I know you ain't ignorant enough to believe that. The bitch is setting your ass up, kid." "Nah I'm feeling her vibe. She ain't playing no games." "Oh yeah and what makes you so sure?" "It was the twinkle in her eye." Jheri had been around the block long enough to know when someone was trying to run game. "Okay let's just say that Padilla was up front. What does that have to do with me?" "It's got everything to do with you. While Padilla was giving me the run down on what she had in mind, the first person I thought about was you. You know that I got skills when it comes to women, but she isn't looking for no ghetto chick. I have been your peeps for a minute and I've seen the way you get the exclusives to fall at your feet and that says a lot about you son".

Jheri stopped short when she realized that Nick wasn't giving her, her full attention. Nick was staring off in the distance. She

40

fully understood the attraction Nick held for Renee. Any nigga would be proud to have a bad ass female like her hanging from their arm. But the question was, was Nick capable of turning Renee out into a life of prostitution? Jheri was confident that once Nick heard the proposal she would run with it.

Nevertheless, she needed Nick's full attention in order to accomplish that. Nick had heard every word, although she acted as though she was not interested in what Jheri had to say - in all reality she was. She would like nothing more than to put her talent to the test. Nick's expertise with the same sex was a gift and she wasn't about to waste it, so there was nothing left for Jheri to say. All she wanted to know was how much her cut was and when should she begin to recruit these ladies. Most of all, she wanted to have a one on one with this Ma'dam C.O. because just a few minutes in her company would allow Nick to know if she was on the up and up. Setting up a meeting between the two shouldn't be too difficult for Jheri.

They needed her, Nick already knew that much. Jheri would make it happen, if the Ma'dam C.O. wanted someone with her skills on her team she would agree to meet with her. Everything depended on their first meeting. Granted, Nick had flair, however there was more to the female species. Not only did a nigga have to satisfy their bodies, she had to satisfy their minds. Quench the thirst most women craved. Criminal thinking most often begins when one is trying to satisfy a need. The objective would be to find out what that need was and then work from there. Jheri looked on as Nick continued to stare off at the baseball field.

"What the fuck you thinking about?" If Jheri could have gotten into Nick's mind, she would find that she already had the women who would be perfect for this venture, women who Jheri wouldn't even consider, and women who Jheri wouldn't look twice at. They were ordinary types who were quiet and shy. The regular dull ones you would probably run into at the local library with their faces buried inside a 300 page book entitled, "The Happy Hooker" by Xavier Hollander. These ordinary types of women always looked for something or someone to add a little spice to their lives. That's where Nick would come in. She knew just the right ingredients to use to make a woman do things they only dreamed of doing. Nick was about to make all of their erotic thoughts become a reality.

"I'm thinking about you setting up a meeting between the Ma'dam C.O. and myself." "I'm not sure if I can do that. She doesn't even know I'm talking to you about this shit." "Oh no," said Nick, now annoyed with Jheri. "Check it son, if you want me to help you get these hoes make this meeting happen. Tell her whatever it is you know she wants to hear and believe me she'll agree." Nick stood up, and then walked away leaving Jheri with something to think about.

Chapter 6

Early the next morning, Déjà went about her daily routine with a huge smile on her face. While she prepared her daughters for school, she told them that life was about to take another turning point. She asked them both what it was they wanted more than anything in the world. Her oldest daughter, Nadiva, danced around the living room saying that she wanted to be a ballerina and her youngest, Brianna, said that she wanted a big house, a dog and lots and lots of Barbie dolls.

Déjà smiled at their innocence. It was a great feeling to know that one day she would be able to give them everything that they deserved. Little did they know she had already rented a place, and luxury was not an option. At the moment the only thing that mattered was that she had found the ideal spot for her whorehouse with the proper climate - cool, discreet, convenient and cheap; not in quality, but in price. It was a perfect two story, ranch style brick house with four bedrooms, two bathrooms, living room, den, family room, kitchen washer and dryer hookup and a two car garage. What had attracted her most to the place was that there was a two bedroom guest house sitting on the property, near a small lake where she envisioned her daughters swimming.

Déjà didn't want her business anywhere near her seeds because subjecting them to her new life would leave a negative effect on them; so what they wouldn't see wouldn't hurt. During the evening hours, while the ladies were in the big house attending to their business, her daughters would be asleep tucked away nice and cozy in the guest house. Déjà thought about hiring a nanny for those evenings when she would have to join the others in their quest.

43

Now that turning her first trick was behind her, she could easily make some extra money on the side. Besides she really enjoyed her sexual experience with Mike Dunn. Her pussy juices had never flowed so freely the way that it did with him. He was well stacked for a white man. Because she had done such an outstanding job in satisfying his needs, Mike had decided long before they left his place that he was going to rent Déjà his own personal home, the home that he shared with his ex-wife and two daughters.

There was a huge For Sale sign standing on the front lawn when they pulled up to his property causing Déjà to glance in his direction confused. She knew that her words at his office were clear; she was only interested in renting a place. She thought that maybe he misunderstood, but he made it clear after a brief discussion that he understood her request clearly. They negotiated on a rental price which was much less then she had anticipated.

Being that Mr. Dunn had been open-minded and accepting of what she wanted the place for, Déjà had promised him free sessions for as long as her business was up and running. Gratitude came in many forms and Déjà showed hers bent over on the cherry wood dining room table Dunn had his meals on long ago. Déjà giggled at the thought of having the Dunn clad walking in on them as he stroked her deeply from behind. What would he do? What would he say? He would have been the one to answer all of their questions because she didn't owe anyone shit and she intended to keep it that way.

"O.k. girls in the truck we're running late!"

"Yeah daddy right there suck that pussy baby. Please don't stop," Devora says as she lifts her hips to meet her lover's mouth. "I'm a cum daddy, oh God that shit feels so good." She continues as her clit begins to ache from the pressure of Nick's tongue rubbing against it. Devora held her thighs up while grabbing the back Nick's head. Then she began to stroke her pussy into her face making the pressure against her clit overpowering.

She couldn't control the chill that ran up and down her spine as she exploded into Nick's mouth. Devora's legs shook uncontrollably along with the rest of her body. Her pussy juices ran down the side of her thighs, and in spite of the over flow it didn't reach further because Nick was right there to catch every drop. That was just round one. Nick was already strapping on her 10"dildo while Devora laid up against her soft down pillows, trying to catch her breath. She waited for Nick to lead the way. Usually her request came in the form of a look or a finger motion. It was pretty unusual that Nick would speak her words out loud. There was no need, her eyes said it all.

Today was different though. Today Devora could see that Nick had something she wanted to say. "Whets wrong daddy. Why are you looking at me like that?" Nick walked over to the black leather lazy boy that sat at the far corner of the room. She stood there for a minute then sat down. Nick's smile was wicked but yet sexy. Her dreads hung to her shoulders, giving

45

her an exotic West Indian look. And the shine, mixed with a little sweat forming around her face excited Devora.

"Spread your legs baby," Nick demanded. As she reached for the nightstand, she pulled the drawer out then reached for a small jar of lubricant. Devora spread her legs wide, exposing her goodies waiting for further instructions.

"Play with yourself," Nick continued to command. Devora placed two fingers into her mouth; she moisturized them with her saliva then began to touch her wetness. Her clit came back to life instantly. The thought of what was going to happen next caused her to moan. She knew that once her daddy pulled out their toy she was in for a night of hot erotic love making. Once Devora reached the point where she could no longer watch Nick stroke her dick with the palm of her hand, she lifted herself up from the bed and walked over to where Nick sat laid back. Her pussy ached, she wanted nothing more than to climb on Nick, position herself just right above her, and then lower herself onto their boy toy. Slowly she spread her legs across Nick's thighs, while one hand stroked her button and the other came around Nick's neck.

"Tell me what you want Daddy," Devora said as she began to lower herself onto Nick's hardness. "I want you to ride me!" "Umm I love it when you talk nasty," Dee whispered. "You do?" "Yes baby I do!"

Together they began to move their hips. Gradually Devora slipped the object into her walls. Sensually she rocked back and forth, moving her pelvic to meet Nick's. Passionately they kissed to near numbness. Nick could feel the wetness between Devora's legs. She could feel the pressure of her movements against her bone. Then something that had never happened before began to happen.

Devora's strokes commenced to hit the tip of her little man in the boat. Her clit was being exposed to Devora's stirs causing it began to throb. Devora was near to everything that was important in Nick's life. With Devora, her woman, her soul mate, everything was just right. They fit like two spoons in a draw. Their bodies glided perfectly against one another. Nick could sense that she wasn't going to be able to hold out any longer. Devora

was a sight for sore eyes, so she attacked Devora's insides, forcing every inch of her dildo into her. Her moans and screams to fuck her just a little bit harder, caused Nick to cum in union with her girl.

"Damn," Nick stated as she stood straight up on her bunk. "What the fuck was that?" "Yo nigga you alright? You sounded like you were having one hell of a dream," One of Nick's twelve room-mates stated. "Yeah dawg. I'm good." "Yeah I bet you are," The roommate smiled at Nick.

The roommate had awoken from the sounds coming from Nick's bed and she began to play with her kitty. Unfortunately Nick woke up before she was able to get off, leaving her high and dry.

Nick swung her legs over to the side of the bed, reached for her roll of toilet paper, then headed for the restroom. There she discovered that she had actually had an orgasm. It felt so real, having Dee spread out over her moaning and calling out her name. For a minute she could have sworn that she was at home buried in between her legs.

"Damn baby I miss the shit out of you," Nick spoke softly to herself as she wiped away the results of what Dee had done to her mental. Devora was one of the main reasons Nick couldn't approach anyone else who had crossed her path. She still loved her, although their relationship had become sour in the past few months, Nick couldn't move on. Her heart and soul belonged to her Spanish Harlem senorita. Memories of how stable their relatetionship was brought tears to Nick's eyes.

It was because of Devora that she now found herself in prison. Dee had been drinking White Russians all evening. The club was packed and the music was pumping. Nick can recall the bartender giving her the heads up on her woman, informing her that Dee had been drinking non-stop and that she was getting a little bit too loose. The plan was for Dee to go to the club directly after work for happy hour, meeting Nick later on in the evening. When Dee didn't show up, Nick had decided to roll through to see what was taking her so long. Luckily she had showed up when she did. Nick headed towards the dance floor in search of her other half. When Dee came into view she found that she had become free of her Liz Claiborne blazer showing off her bustier. Half naked Devora danced seductively against someone else.

Enraged by her hoe-ish behavior, Nick ran up on her grabbing, her by the arm and pulling her away from the dance floor and the stranger who now had his hands all over her ass. Everything happened in slow motion from that point on. The stranger spoke, violating Nick's place as Devora's lover.

"Yo what the fuck are you doing? Don't you see that the young lady and I were getting into something serious?" The stranger then placed his hand on Nick's shoulder. Nick quickly turned around then shoved the stranger off of her. "The only thing you're going to get into is a coffin!"
Nick couldn't remember anything that happened after that. She went completely blank. All she knew was that when she had come to, she had been handcuffed and escorted out of the club by two Police Officers. Dee's cries could be heard from a distance, however nothing else registered.

Since that evening Nick's life had taken a turn for the worse. Devora was not taking care of her business the way she was suppose to, putting a huge strain on their relationship. Nick didn't know from one day to the next where she stood in Dee's life, killing her spirit on a daily basis. Who else could she trust, if her own woman was shitting on her. All of her questions would be answered though once she was released. Devora had some explaining to do. That much was for sure.

Chapter 7

Jheri waited patiently by the officers' bubble as Déjà recorded her daily activities into her log book. It was 7: 30 am and already Jheri had a hard on. Déjà's femininity created desires in her groin. Despite the different roles they played, Jheri craved to have Déjà wrapped around her waist. Déjà noticed the little sneak peaks coming from Jheri. She was flattered, however she choose to ignore her advances. She only had one purpose for Jheri. Jheri was to recruit the females she needed - that was it and that was all. If in fact Jheri had any other ideas, when it came to her, she had better think again.

Déjà planned on keeping their relationship on a professional level. Sure, she found Jheri attractive, however her goods were up for trade. If she wanted someone outside of the industry, she would be the one choosing. Déjà didn't have time for no one who held a child like crash on her and she sure as hell wasn't going to be chosen by someone who didn't fit the category. It was all about the Benjamin's; cash money is all Déjà wanted to feel flowing. Besides she wasn't gay and she wasn't about to succumb to Jheri's flirtatious ways. It was better to nip Jheri's fantasy of her in the bud now before things got out of hand, Déjà concluded as she scribbled a few more words into her log book, and then turned around to give Jheri her full attention.

"What's up," Déjà questioned Jheri with attitude. "I need to talk to you," she answered back with the same tone. "Alright let's go out here." Déjà walked out of the dorm area, heading for the front porch. Two minutes later they were standing outside with cigarettes dangling from their mouths.

"Listen I hollered at one of my niggas and she is down for whatever." "So what's the problem," Déjà snapped. "Ain't no problem why don't you let a nigga speak." Quickly Déjà apologized. She had realized that she needed to be easy. It was the stares coming from Jheri that placed her in an uncomfortable position.

"You alright? You seem to be under a lot of mental strain?" Jheri dealt with women on a daily basis and she was conscious of how moody they can be. Downplaying the situation Jheri decided to start practicing on her new characteristics. By catching the bees you had to have a whole lot of honey.

"Nah I'm alright, just a few things I got to take care of." Déjà had second thoughts about checking Jheri. Maybe it wasn't such a bad idea that Jheri was attracted to her. It may benefit her in the long run. Hopefully it would make Jheri work that much harder towards her goals.

"I hear that shawty. Anyway my partner requested to see you, talk with you a little, so that she can get a better perception of your plan," Jheri stated now moving in towards the Ma'dam C.O.

"I'm not sure if I should do that," Déjà whispered into Jheri's ear. "The less people I meet, the better it would be. You understand that my job can be on the line." Déjà expressed, as her warm breath tickled the hairs on Jheri's neck.

"Yeah I understand. But if you want your scheme to work I'm going to need some assistance." "You are, are you?" Déjà moved in a little closer causing Jheri to step back. "Yeah." "I hear you baby boy but do you trust this friend of yours?" "Most definitely." "Why?" "Why what?" "Why do you trust this person so much?"

"Why you asking me so many questions. I thought you wanted me to do what I had to do," Jheri stated with confusion in her voice. "I do. However you must, and listen to me carefully Jheri. You must know at all times who you are dealing with. Don't ever take a needed hand as a sure sign of loyalty. You can misread someone else's intentions, which can cause you to make one of the biggest mistakes of your life. I have no room for mistakes!" Déjà meant what she said. Vulnerability within the P-Nile can also cause someone who might have had good judgment out on the streets to become misguided.

"Do you understand, Jheri that I can't afford to make my presence known just yet?" "I can respect that shawty, unfortunately you ain't got much of a choice. Trust and believe me that if you're looking for high profile dick stoppers, my man is the one who could make that happen," Jheri stated with a devious grin.

"She must be one hell of a charmer." "No doubt." "Alright, I'll tell you what. Give me a minute to think about it." "That's fair

53

enough," Jheri said before she stepped away from their conference. Then on a chance she stated "You won't regret it!"

Meanwhile, back in C-block, Nick jumped into the shower, in hopes of washing away her delayed reaction. The dream had become so real that when she was about to reach an orgasm she actually did, making Nick a little disappointed in herself. She felt that she should have had control over her emotions, but it wasn't easy when a nigga was in love. Nick turned the shower knob to adjust the water temperature, cooling off the heat that ran throughout her bare skin. She felt like she was on fire. Devora's face came into view as she closed her eyes. Nick wished that she could just forget how good Devora had made her feel. Nick had lost the battle a long time ago.

She believed that she had found the perfect woman, hard working, beautiful, conservative in the streets but scandalous in the sheets, a true freak by nature. Devora was the reason why she had given up the street life. Slinging crack cocaine on the corners of Albany, New York had not produced the rush that Devora did. So when Devora asked Nick to change her profession, she didn't hesitate.

Finding a new occupation had been the easy part. It was the hours that had affected her the most. Waking up early in the morning to punch a time clock had caused Nick difficulty. Although it had been a struggle in the beginning, considering the fact that Nick never had a job before. Her mind and body had fallen into a healthy routine, with no worries of ever being robbed on a street corner by her so called friends, nor ever having to worry about getting arrested for the sale of a controlled substance.

Nick honestly believed that she had been one of the lucky ones, great job, and beautiful home with an exquisite wife. All three had definitely been a blessing from God. Yet like a thief in the night, the enemy (devil) snatched it away. The cold water had become unbearable on Nick's shoulders causing her body temperature had come down immensely, enough for Nick to go on about her day as though nothing had accrued during her sleeping hours. Nick didn't need any interruptions from Devora.

Her mind needed to be free from anything passionate. After what Jheri had proposed, Nick's mind would convert back to the days when she didn't feel love, happiness, or loyalty for anyone. If indeed Jheri was serious about what this C.O had professed, Nick was about to embark onto a new adventure. Taking what had naturally been given to her at birth and using it to the best of her ability.

"Wright, report to the bubble (officer's station)". Déjà ordered into the intercom. "Yeah what's up Padilla," Jheri asked as she approached the C.O's station. "Make it happen," Déjà said. "I'll be working a double. I don't know where I'll be posted yet, so just keep your eyes and ears open." "That's what's up," Jheri said as she winked at Déjà. That wink would come to mean many different things for many different reasons.

Chapter 8

Six months later...

That's how it all began, Déjà reminisced as she now stood in front of the perfume counter at Bergdorf Goodman. Life had become luxurious, being able to come to New York City on a shopping spree once a week was one of her favorite pass times. Dressed impeccably in a Giorgio Armani black off the shoulder mini dress, black patent leather ankle-wrap pumps designed by Yves Saint Laurent, and a full length black mink sable, Déjà had been welcomed along with her long money, into the many high fashioned boutiques that lined up Madison Avenue.

Today she had planned on hitting a few places like Chanel and Louis Vuitton; Bergdorf Goodman had not been on her agenda, but she couldn't resist once she glanced towards their display window and found that they were selling a new line of perfume by Christian Dior. Déjà entered their brass doors with grace.

Having money had brought her to new heights, where once she felt that she had to work twice as hard to achieve her goal, now she just laid back and reaped the benefits of her investments. Renee, Destiny, Jamie, Shaun, Angie and Nicole played their parts effortlessly; everything she taught them about the escort service had come naturally. It was no wonder that her stable of ladies did an amazing job of keeping the money pouring in. Just as she had requested, Jheri and Nick had chosen the ladies successfully converting them from their prior professions.

Once Nick and Jheri went to work, one by one had agreed to the terms the fellas' had brought forth. The girls basically recruited themselves; after one brief conversation with Renee Destiny followed, together they had decided on the arrangements. Once released from prison they would have found themselves back on the block doing the same old thing. So getting back into the con game wasn't a problem it was the consequences they could have done without. Basically when they were offered new living arrangements along with educational opportunities in whatever field they were interested, in they signed their names on the dotted line. All the others were already in the sex industry in one form or another making it easy for Nick and Jheri to recruit them.

Jamie, a 21 year old Asian girl, who worked as a dancer at Club Ecstasy, had come across a gentleman who had requested a lap dance in the V.I.P section of the club. Once they were in one of the private rooms, Jamie asked the gentleman to pay her up front; since he had been a regular at the club he became offended. Although she traded her goodies for funds Jamie had a goal to fulfill - she had a lifelong dream of going to college and getting a degree in the Arts. She knew that she would fit in amongst the other students. With an alcoholic mother and a dope fiend father, Jamie had learned quickly as a child that wearing different faces was essential to her survival. She had to learn to transform herself according to their moods. Drama instructors couldn't possibly have anything on her parents.

Shaun is a 23 year old Jamaican girl from Brooklyn, who unlike Jamie, came from a respectable highly regarded prestigious family. Her parents were both in the medical profession and they worked long hours building a private clinic. Leaving little to no time for their daughter, Shaun began to look for comfort in the arms of the many men who crossed her path.

Somewhere along the way she was acquainted with another young lady who introduced her to the escort service where she began to indulge in the sex industry. Selling her pussy for a price brought an edge to what she already enjoyed doing. Shaun was in it for the enjoyment, so the money she received was just an added bonus. When asked by Nick what career moves she was interested in, she simply said nothing.

Angie is a 19 year old mixed breed; her Indian and Puerto Rican blood lines made her one very spiritual young lady. She too enjoyed exploring her femininity. Angie believed that there was no other way to get in touch with her inner being than by the joining of two souls. Her techniques in the bedroom caused her, as well as her partners, to have outer body experiences. This had cemented Angie's career choice to become a marriage counselor.

Nicole had been the most problematic because she had been a renegade at 20 years old. She had refused to be controlled by pimps while she was out working the streets of Hunts Points.

She felt strongly about selling her goods; it was a means to an end for her, a way to survive to pay rent, buy food, and support her two year old son, who now lived with her mother in the South Bronx. Her sassy attitude had caused Nick to work her charm on overdrive. Nevertheless, Nicole paid attention to what Nick had to say. She could not deny that the offer Nick proposed was one she could live with. Nicole loved her independence, so her career choice was Marketing.

As each girl arrived at Déjà's establishment which she named Butterflies, she made it a point to personally welcome them, assuring them that everything promised by Nick and Jheri had been on the up and up. The first thing Déjà did was introduce herself as their new employer, and then she moved to a brief interview as she

showed them around the premises. While she conducted the tour, Déjà observed the ladies as they sashayed beside her. Appearance was most important when working in an establishment such as Déjà's because quality had to come hand in hand with quantity. Therefore her guidelines would not be compromised by trashy behavior.

After the tour, Déjà had taken them to a small room in the back of the house that she used as a study. There Déjà filled out the necessary paper work the ladies would need to receive Federal Student Aid. Being that before their release from prison they were required to send for their birth certificates and social security cards, all that was left for them to do was to obtain I.D from the Department of Motor Vehicles and, fill out the applications necessary for student funding and finally registering for classes at the community college. Once all of the educational stuff was said and done, Déjà went into the Occupational aspect. She explained to each young lady that their source of livelihood was going to be the true success of Butterflies. Their dedication and commitment to the life would determine their future.

A sales woman watched as Déjà stood by the perfume display. Déjà was in such a deep trance that the sales lady did not want to disturb her. There was a unique twinkle in Déjà's eyes that couldn't go unnoticed. The sales woman depended on the commissions she made from her customers and she knew that Déjà was going to purchase something, so the sales woman did not budge. It was as though Déjà's glow was payment enough. She would have done anything to have the same look on her face. Someone or something was definitely making the woman before her very happy. "That look was priceless," the sales woman thought as she continued to watch closely.

Déjà slowly came out of her trance. Memories of Butterflies' grand opening had also come to mind, however she didn't have time to stand around and think about it. Déjà reached for the sampler, sprayed a few drops onto her wrist, and then glanced at the wall to wall mirror that framed the Christian Dior counter. Before she was able to get a whiff of the fragrance she observed the brass doors opening behind her. In walked a handsomely looking creature, dressed in a black Dolce & Gabbana full length leather trench coat. Through the creatures black shades, Déjà's noticed that their eyes flickered back and forth as though looking for someone. The scene intrigued her because it reminded her of the movie The Matrix. The black Keanu Reeves was something to write home about; any woman would be proud to indulge in such a fine specimen.

Déjà smiled as she thought of herself as being that woman. When the person found what they were looking for, they began to move forward. Strolling down the red carpet that covered the main floor of Bergdorf Goodman they appeared to be upset. The attitude just added to their sex appeal making Déjà feel a tinkle of her pussy juices drip down her inner thigh. She wiggled her legs together hoping to distract her kitty from going places she didn't want to go. Déjà continued to stare into the mirror, watching as the creature got closer.

Suddenly she found that the person was standing directly behind her. No words were exchanged because Déjà knew exactly who this creature was, so she just went in for the kill by applying her lips onto the individual. She slipped her tongue into the person's mouth, all the while making love to the full soft lips. Nick slowly traced her hand down the front of Déjà's dress then slipped her hand underneath it.

"Are you happy to see me girl or is all that wetness for somebody else?" Nick lifted her fingers to her mouth to taste her. "All of that is for you Daddy." "Prove it to me." "Here? Now?" "Yeah show me how happy you are." "Baby stop playing." Déjà playfully bit her bottom lip. "Who's playing?" "Umm you are so nasty," Déjà said as she then spread her legs a little wider. She lifted her mini dress so that Nick could stroke her clit slightly.

Her crouch less panties were one of Nick's favorite accessorizes. She insisted that Déjà buy a few pairs from the pussy cat shop on one of their trips to the village, knowing that Nick was spontaneous like that she began to wear them on the regular.

"You are such a good girl baby whose pussy is that?" "Yours." "Oh yeah?" "Yeah," Déjà whispered into Nick's ear as she held on to Nick's shoulders with both hands. Once Déjà reached her climax ,she looked over her own shoulder and winked at the sales lady who stood by watching.

Chapter 9

Déjà and Nick walked down 5th Avenue without a care in the world. As the world past them by, they held hands, cuddled and stopped in the middle of the street to kiss. People walked by making comments as they observed the lovers embrace. "I know that's right girl," one lady said before she stepped off the curb to cross the street. A gentleman came up from behind them and stated." You go my brother let that woman know how much she's worth," as he too disappeared into the crowd of pedestrians. That statement made both Déjà and Nick stop dead in their tracks. They both looked at each other and burst out laughing.

Anyone who looked at Nick from a distance automatically assumed that she was a man due to her strong physique and demeanor. They both liked that people could be fooled so easily, making Déjà that much more comfortable in her love affair. Nick intoxicated her in every way. Yeah, she could recall the days when she used to say that she wasn't gay and that she would never go there. However things were different now. She loved everything about being with Nick - the way that she walked, talked, and her intellect. Yeah, her sex appeal was an asset too; it was the way Nick made her coochie jump for joy whenever she was about to have an intense orgasm. No one has ever touched Déjà's nookie the way that Nick did. She knew just where to go without any guidance, but there was one problem Déjà just couldn't come up with a solution for.

Their affair was a secret, something Nick did not approve of. Of course if Déjà was in her shoes she probably wouldn't like it either. Although Déjà had felt that it was for the best, Nick was not happy with their arrangement. Déjà felt that her primary responsibility was to her business, "Butterflies," and to the ladies who worked for her. She refused to allow herself to be moved by Nick's feelings. There was just too much at stake. In the past six months since Butterflies opening, Déjà had filled her little black book with some of the biggest names in Corrections. D.O.C had become Déjà's biggest clients. The atmosphere at Butterflies was soft and comforting making the establishment a big hit. Security is what the men who entered her doors every night looked for. Because of their status what these gentlemen did behind closed doors had to be kept strictly confidential. Although all of the men received the same courtesy, D.O.C's men were treated like royalty. Most of these men had become an asset to the trade, especially the ones who were higher up on the ladder like the Superintendents, Captains and Lieutenants. Not only were they the ones who the ladies had to keep happy, they were also the one's Déjà had to keep an eye on.

If she didn't learn anything from her relationship with her ex-husband, she learned to always be two steps ahead of her opponent. They could make and break you with a blink of an eye. A risk Déjà was willing, yet cautious, to take. This is one of the main reasons why she couldn't allow Nick in too deep. Their arrangement was pretty simple, and wanting more wouldn't benefit either one of them at the moment. Staying focused was the key to making Déjà's business successful, even though Déjà was completely engrossed in her business she still found time to play.

Whenever she needed to get away from the hustle and bustle of selling coochie, Nick was the one that she would turn to. Nick definitely knew how to melt away all of the stress she faced throughout the day. There was no question that didn't go unanswered when Nick was smoothing out all of her rough spots. The way that Nick took the time to care for her every need, made Déjà keep going back for more. She was addicted since day one. Thinking back now at how their affair began, Déjà grabbed Nick by the hand and then said, "Baby do you still remember our first encounter?" "Of course I do, you almost jumped out of your clothes when you saw me," Nick smiled teasing Déjà. "Oh really! I don't remember it quite like that."

"So tell me sexy lady how do you remember our first encounter," Nick asked as she moved in bringing Déjà's back against a brick wall. "Well baby I was hoping you would tell me," Déjà responded breathing deeply into Nick's mouth. "Oh I know what you want. You want daddy to tell you a story." "Yeah something like that." Nick leaned in, then turned Déjà's head to the side and began to whisper into her ear.

"It all started like this. I walked into the chapel library at Albion and there at the front desk sitting down on a black swivel chair with both feet up on the desk and crossed at the ankles was you, by the way very sexy ankles," Nick emphasized as she tickled Déjà's earlobe with her tongue. "I noticed your ankle bracelet and the way that it hugged your smooth delicate skin. It was an instant turn on for me to watch you sitting there. Then my eyes traveled up your body in search of something else that would convince me to go forward with this crazy idea of yours. Your curves underneath the uniform you wore pulled me further into that room. Girl you were not at all what I was expecting to see. You made a nigga want to tear every piece of that bondage off of you just to see if what you had underneath was real. You are so perfectly put together. God broke the mold when he created you, baby."

Déjà couldn't help how her pussy juices flowed from the sound of Nick's voice. She felt a little tremble inside of her canal. Her eyes had been roaming the streets hoping that maybe she could play with her kitty as Nick continued with her story. "Anyway I had to be easy because Jheri had already put me on to your style. But that wasn't enough for me; I had to see for myself. I'm glad that I did put the pressure on. That first day was something out of a porno flick. We about lost our minds down there in that room. Do you remember that girl?" Déjà shook her head up and down in a yes motion.

"Even though I was five minutes late you seemed to have an aura about you. You were just sitting back relaxing listening to one of those corny ass radio stations. You also had a magazine up in your face acting like I hadn't entered the room. But you knew I was there right? Cause you heard me breathing. Your perfume mixed with your natural scent filled that room Déjà. You smelled so good mami. Damn, I couldn't help myself when I moved forward to meet you. You didn't even recognize that you were no longer in that little room all by yourself did you? It was as though you were waiting for me to speak first. You felt my presence right baby?"

Nick had to take a deep breath before she was able to continue. Her private body parts had come to life. Nick adjusted her pants then pressed her bone against Déjà's and continued.

"Slowly you lowered the magazine looked me straight in the eye and said, "you're late." There was something about the way you looked at me that made me want you right there on the spot. I felt like all of my energy had been drained out of my body. Your eyes were so mesmerizing. Slowly you lowered your legs, sat up straight in your chair, and then asked me to come closer. I didn't know what you were thinking because you just sat there looking at me up and down as though I was an item up for sale. I could tell that you were very nervous … maybe even a little scared. You were fidgeting around in your seat."

"That's because my pussy was drenched," Déjà explained as she began to stroke her pussy against Nick's. "Oh yeah?" "Mmm hmm," Déjà licked her lips. "Anyway I walked towards you, by passing the desk and everything else that stood between us. Once I found myself directly in front of you, I reached up, grabbed you by the back of your neck then went in for the kill with a long passionate kiss. Baby you opened your mouth like a good little girl, then stuck your tongue down my throat," Nick chuckled, and then continued.

"Your mouth was so hot. There must have been pent-up heat inside of you. I could tell that your body had been deprived of any real sexual satisfaction." "You are so right baby." "I know I am." "When I realized what you were asking for, I went into butch mode, lifting you up onto the desk after I lowered your pants and unbutton your shirt, I kissed your breast feeding off of the energy you released. Your nipples became rock hard in my mouth as I sucked them gently. Mami, I watched your facial expressions the whole time. You're eyes closed then your head fell back in ecstasy. I watched you as you inserted two of your fingers into your mouth moisturizing them with your saliva. Then you glided your fingertips down the front of your body towards your kitty. Baby you stroked your clit softly bringing it to its full erection. It was such a pretty sight. I could smell your juices seeping out of you. You smelled so delicious. I allowed you to reach your first orgasm as I watched. I've seen so many women masturbate, but you did it in such a way that I too had to touch myself."

Nick noticed that while she was getting deeper into her story, Déjà's hand had found its way into her pants. Déjà's finger touched Nick's clit in slow circular motions. That's one of the many things she loved about Déjà - she wasn't afraid to show her freaky side. It didn't matter where they were at, what Déjà wanted Déjà got.

"Stroke it baby. Make your daddy cum." "Oh I plan to." "I was dying to get in between your walls. You were making me lose my mind." "I wanted you so bad," Déjà whispered back. "I know that's why I lowered myself onto the seat threw your legs over my shoulders and began to French kiss your nookie. Your body shivered with every twist of my tongue. Baby you brought your pelvic bone up to me then you laid down across the desk with your arms over your head. You rose to the occasion with your moves. I wanted to get inside of you girl. To feel the muscles of your walls squeeze. You grabbed for my hand, and pulled it towards your pussy. You wanted me to finger fuck you, so I did. First I put one finger, two, and then three and of course the rest followed. You opened up real wide for me. I could have gone for more but I didn't want to hurt you. It had been a long time since I considered someone else feelings. Mami, you danced on my hand, your eyes became misty as you lifted yourself onto your elbows and looked at me. The flavor of your flow was all over my mouth. I wanted you to taste it, so I stood up, leaned over and kissed you while I fucked you deeply. I knew I was hitting your g-spot because you were moaning so loudly. Your screams became louder and your body jerked with each motion. Do you remember that baby?"

"Yes I do that was one of the best orgasms I ever had." "I wanted to fill you completely. When I felt that you was about to cum I took my fingers out of your pussy to replace them with my mouth I wanted every drop of you. You exploded so profoundly that your flow dripped down the side of my lips." "Did I taste good," Déjà asked as she continued to stroke Nick.

71

"Yeah baby you tasted good." "How about you give me the same? Can I taste you baby," Déjà asked.

Nick opened her trench giving her the go ahead. Déjà lowered herself to her knees. She unbuckled Nick's belt opened her pants then kissed Nick's box, she licked it softly, nibbling on it gently until she felt Nick's body Jerk from her movements. There in the middle of midtown N.Y. on a brick wall Déjà made love to Nick until she released herself all over her mouth.

Chapter 10

Déjà turned onto the circular driveway that led up to her house. The rubble underneath the tires of her Range Rover reminded her of the sound of pebbles being thrown into a running river. It was a sound she welcomed whenever Butterflies was open for business. During the evening hours that sound had alerted her of the clients who arrived for a night of pleasure. She noticed that the establishment was dimly lit and that every room in the house was occupied, a sign that her ladies were dedicated to their profession. Déjà was happy to know that she didn't have to be there every minute of the day in order for her operation to run smoothly.

Once a week, before Déjà took her trips into the city, she would choose one of the ladies to manage the place for a few hours. Today she had chosen Destiny, and from the look of things Destiny was doing a great job of keeping the ladies busy. Walking through the front door with Nick closely behind, Déjà called out informing Destiny of her arrival, "Destiny!" "Yeah," Destiny hollered back as she walked towards Déjà. "Its YES Destiny. What have I told you about your vocabulary," Déjà stood sternly. "Yes ma'dam," Destiny corrected herself while looking at Déjà and Nick. "So how was your trip," Destiny asked as she grabbed the shopping bags out of Déjà's hand. She knew that on Déjà's trips into New York City she explored her essences.

All of the ladies knew that her trips were more than just shopping sprees; it was the way that Nick kept a close eye on her that made their relationship obvious. "It was great and also exhausting. How is everything here?" Déjà quickly removed her pumps and patted down the hall towards her office. Destiny followed quietly behind her. She placed the bags down in a corner then sat down across from Déjà. Déjà slowly lowered herself onto her seat then looked at the monitors that hung to the side of her.

"I see that business is good, all of the rooms are full." "Yes ma'am." "Why aren't you working?" "I just finished pleasing one of our customers." "Oh really who," Déjà questioned Destiny with a smile on her face. Déjà loved to hear those words. The more pussy they sold the more money she made. "Sergeant Anderson stopped by before going home to his lovely wife and kids." Destiny now lit a cigarette she had inserted into a solid gold holder. "Isn't it amazing how the same men you dealt with on a daily basis in the prison system, you now deal with as clients in the free world." "Yes, although I still can't seem to get use to the idea of fucking individuals who I despise." "I'm sure that they must feel the same way. But like the great Tina Turner said, "What's love got to do with it?""

"I guess you're right. Besides once I'm in hoe mode these people don't have a face. All I'm interested in, are the faces on those Benjamin's their tossing my way." "Now that's what I want to hear. So tell me how much have the ladies made today," Déjà asked while still keeping an eye on the video

74

display. Destiny reached into her high thigh boots and pulled out the cash that she had just charged for one of her dominatrix episodes. "Here is $500.00 the rest is in your sterling silver music box that's under your desk."

Déjà slowly pushed her chair back a little as she bent down to retrieve one of her greatest possessions. The sterling silver box had been a gift from her daughter Nadiva. Once everything was in place and the movers had left Déjà called out to her daughter. "Yes mommy," Nadiva answered as she held the silver music box in her hand. "What are you doing up there." Déjà had decided to go up to the attic and investigate.

At the top of the landing Déjà found her daughter sitting in front of an old wooden chest. Nadiva had been mesmerized by the way the light shined off the bits of glass that laid across the top. "What do you have there Nadiva?" "It's a box mommy. Isn't it pretty?" Déjà bent over to get a closer look and she too had become taken with the box. "That is so beautiful let mommy see that." Déjà reached out her hand and Nadiva handed it over as though she had found a treasure.

"It looks like a music box." She opened the top and like she had suspected the box came to life. The melody was not familiar; however mother and daughter were tempted to sing along. "Mommy, you can have it if you want." "I can, can I?" "Yes it's pretty just like you and I want to give it to you." Nadiva jumped up and wrapped her little arms around Déjà's neck making that the second most important day between mother and daughter; the first naturally was the day that Nadiva was born.

75

Since then Déjà kept the music box on her desk using it as a reminder of better days to come. With the box now in her hand, Déjà placed it gently onto her desk top, opened it and reached for the wad of bills. She began to count it as she continued to glance at the cameras; she counted out $5000.00 dollars, making Déjà was pleased.

"You ladies have done well tonight," Déjà smiled wickedly. "Thank you ma'am." Meanwhile in one of the upstairs rooms, Shaun was putting in the final touches with a lethal stroke, causing the gentleman who laid underneath her to jerk his body violently reaching his climax. Holding Shaun tightly by the waist, he dug deeper into her tunnel one last time hoping that she would feel his fury.

Unfortunately that wasn't the case; where once she sincerely enjoyed sex, now she was disgusted by it. Maybe it was because back then, before she committed herself to Déjà and Butterflies, she picked and choose who she wanted to share her body with. In this type of business the women couldn't choose their mate. They had a part to play and with that came a price, so choosing was not an option. Shaun dreaded the times when the doorbell rang. She sometimes became frightened of what was on the other side. Although 90% of Déjà's clients were respectful, being distinguished in the way that they handled their business, the other 10% were into all kinds of freaky shit Shaun was not accustom to.

Nevertheless, Shaun performed her duties willingly due to the five hundred dollars an hour she received. It was tricks like the

76

one she now performed on that turned her stomach. Bald headed 5 foot'11 inches tall, 250 lbs, with a body odor strong enough to knock out all of western New York. His little dick wasn't up to par either, Sergeant Wilcox really thought that he was doing something with his little object. Then to make matters worse, he wanted his full hour's worth of pussy. Shaun just wasn't up to pleasing a man without getting some type of pleasure herself. One of her main reasons for signing on with Déjà was to fuck her brains out without the inconvenience of having to go out of her way to find partners. Secondly, she thought, "why not kill two birds with one stone; fuck and get paid."

She still hadn't decided what she wanted to do as far a career was concerned, so Déjà just stashed Shaun's money, until she made her choice. While all of the other women went off to college everyday, Shaun just stayed back and enjoyed the comforts of being alone. Those early hours went to shopping, getting her nails and feet done by the only nail salon in Albion. Then she would roam the grounds, clueless as to what she wanted to do with the rest of her life. Shaun knew that selling herself wasn't going to be a lifetime gig.

Some days were worst than others and today was one of the bad days. After Sergeant Wilcox did his deed, Shaun jumped off of him with quickness. He had sensed that Shaun was irritated by the way that she held her body back from him. He had become annoyed with her new and improved attitude. The more she held back, the more pressure he put on her to give him his monies' worth because he was not willing to get jerked for five hundred dollars of his hard earned cash. Like it or not she was going to work. Isn't that what she was, a working girl?

"So why all the drama," Sergeant Wilcox thought to himself as he began to dress. The Sergeant watched as Shaun rushed to the restroom and closed the door behind her, where he could hear the running water from the shower. Anger began to emerge from her actions. He felt that she could have at least told him how great of a lover he was like she use to, and that she would love for him to come back and give her some more of his big fat dick. The last few times that they were together Shaun seemed to know exactly what to say to boost up his ego. He knew that what he was holding between his legs wasn't enough to satisfy most women, but Shaun, on the other hand, made him feel as though he held the Holy Grail. This is why he had chosen her time after time. Shaun did things to his manhood that no other woman had been able to accomplish.

Dressing quickly he decided to confront her. He waited patiently in the room. Déjà had noticed most of the moves on the camera. When she zoomed in closer to get a better look at the Sergeant she noticed that he seemed bothered by something. Their session had been over and she couldn't figure out why he was just sitting on Shaun's ottoman with his arms folded over his chest.

"Destiny how long has Sergeant Wilcox been here?" "Oh, he's been here for over an hour." Destiny stood up now as she walked over to the monitors. "What's wrong with this picture

Destiny?" "He looks pissed the fuck off." "The question is why?" "Ma'dam I don't see Shaun." "She's in the bathroom." "Do you want me to go up there and check it out?" "Nah I'll do it." Déjà stood up then headed to Shaun's bedroom.

Chapter 11

Destiny stood quietly watching the monitors. Rooms one thru five were still in full swing. Business was definitely good. Renee was bent over at the waist getting her freak on from behind. Jamie was licking her tricks instrument as he exploded into her mouth. Angie had just finished masturbating for her John and Nicole was lying on her back like a true pillow queen. "Everything is ok there," Destiny thought as she pushed down on the panel of buttons.

The cameras began to move towards Déjà's direction. Destiny had to admire her ma'dam's grace. She had a unique style about herself that one couldn't help but to envy. The way that she climbed the stairs would make someone who didn't know the true story behind Butterflies believe that Déjà was born into the royal family. True elegance was one of her better characteristics.

Destiny had often wondered how it would feel to be able to walk in Déjà's shoes. Déjà sensed that she was being watched so she looked up into one of the hidden cameras and winked. "Destiny was a natural at the job; always on point with matters of the household," Déjà thought to herself as she continued to climb up the steps. She walked down the hall and knocked on Shaun's door. No one answered but she could hear voices coming from inside. Over time the voices became louder and disturbing. She could hear Shaun arguing with the sergeant, expressing her annoyance at finding him still in the room after their session had been over. Suddenly Déjà heard a deep groan, followed by a loud noise as though someone had fallen. Before she was able to retrieve her keys from her pocket the screams coming from Shaun had pierced throughout the house. Every door on the second floor flew open, and Renee, Jamie, Angie and Nicole hurriedly ran down the hall in the direction of Shaun's room. Déjà quickly opened the door afraid of what she may find, nevertheless she had to investigate. For six months Butterflies had been running smoothly, but there was no doubt in Déjà's mind that one day she or one of the ladies would come across some problems. A dissatisfied customer was more in her line of thinking. She never thought that violence would be a factor at her establishment. Clients were screened thoroughly before they were allowed to part take in any activity, so safety had never been Déjà's concern. Being that most of her clients were Government Officials, she neglected to take that into consideration. Now as she stood at the door frame with her mouth open, she realized she had made a huge mistake. First she looked at Shaun who was standing in the middle of the room completely nude holding a small black jack in her hand, hypnotized by the blood that sprayed out of the Sergeant's head. Shaun's breathing was shallow and she was foaming at the mouth. Déjà then gazed down at Sergeant Wilcox's body, who seemed not to be breathing at all. There was no sign of life, just dead weight. Angie was the first to enter. Moving Déjà slightly over to the side, Angie took a deep breath and walked over to Shaun. Softly she said Shaun's name but didn't get a response.

Destiny continued to stare at the cameras in Déjà's office, she was stuck. She could not believe what had just taken place. In the background she could here Nick and Jheri running up the steps. They too heard Shaun's screams from the basement where Nick was giving Jheri the 411 on her trip to the City. Angie spoke softly, careful not to trigger any more violence from Shaun. "Shaun." No response. Shaun remained in the center of her bedroom gasping for air. Traumatized by what she had just done she began to withdraw mentally. Shaun heard Angie speak her name, but she couldn't activate her vocal cords. Her mind set was completely off balance and she couldn't bring herself to speak. Drenched in her own sweat, she felt the metal object slip from her hand and onto the floor.

Déjà and the rest of the ladies stood by, closely taking in the shocking and devastating scene. Angie bent down over the Sergeant's body, placing her index and middle finger onto the side of his neck in search of a pulse. She found that although it was very weak there was one. Looking back over her shoulder she informed Déjà that the Sergeant was still alive. Then she reached out to grab metal black jack when suddenly Nick yelled out before storming into the room, "Don't touch that Angie!" "What the fuck," Jheri questioned as she hurriedly rushed into the bedroom too. "Yo Yo chill nigga." Nick held her hand out stopping Jheri in her tracks. Angie stood up so abruptly she almost lost her balance. Luckily Nick was standing over her, giving her the leverage she needed to stand on her own two feet. Renee was next to enter the room. Looking around from side to side she searched for one of Shaun's

83

robes. With none in sight Renee quickly took the sheets off the bed and threw it gently over Shaun's shoulders.

"Shaun baby what happened," Renee asked as she came around with the sheet covering the front of Shaun's body. Renee uttered the same question to Déjà who remained standing in the doorway. Renee held Shaun in her arms waiting for the lady boss to say something. Nick too stood patiently waiting for Déjà to play her position. This was her place, her clients, so it was her decision. Déjà's mind went into overdrive. Visions of her past came into play. The abuse she had put up with for so long was suppressed, until now. Once Déjà walked out of her marriage and her home Déjà also placed those miserable memories behind her. Seeing Shaun in her tormented state of mind, took Déjà back to that last night when her so called husband, the man she once loved and trusted, almost beat her to death. With swollen eyes, and busted nose and lips Déjà grabbed her daughters and a few of their personal belongings then headed towards a safe haven. Nick immediately noticed that Déjà was trapped someplace in her thoughts. Nicole walked over to her, "Ma'dam what's wrong?" "Yo Déjà, why the fuck are you just standing there," Jheri hollered. "She looks spaced out; wave your hand in front of her eyes Nicole," Angie ordered as she also walked in Déjà direction. "Nah leave her alone. I'll take care of it." Nick grabbed Angie by the arm pulling her back. "Take your fuckin hands off of me Nick. Don't make me spazz out in this motherfucka. That's the problem with niggas, now they don't know how to keep their hands to themselves." Angie tossed her

84

hand up swinging them from side to side. Nick raised her hand up too but not for the reason Angie may have thought; she raised her hands to surrender. Nicole took Déjà by the shoulders and began to shake her. Her words were soft but firm.

There was no time for any bullshit, so they had to come up with something quick. If Sergeant Wilcox was indeed still alive he would be coming out of it soon. By the time he woke up from his unconscious state, Déjà would have to be ready to deal. "Déjà, listen girl, you have to step up to the plate. You're the only one who can take care of this!" "Yes ma'dam please come back. Damn where the fuck are you? What, did you take a trip without the luggage? Déjà come on."

Nicole looked back at the others hoping that they would know what to do. Jamie stood quietly taking in her surroundings. Everyone seemed to be in a state of hysteria, something she was used to seeing around her parent's home. She remembered how her father would become hysterical or go into shock whenever he ran out of his fix; it was a serious diagnosis with withdrawal muscle spasms and sometimes even violence. He would talk them through his state of denial; assuring them that everything could be taken care of through a bag of good heroin or the old fashioned methadone. Treatments from a nearby clinic were so advanced nowadays that 9 times out of 10 he would come out of it a winner. All of that sounded good to them. Jamie's parents had taken an oath, a formal promise to themselves, as drugs addicts, to be the best at what they did. But in this case none of that mattered. Jamie too had taken an oath. Her formal promise was to get paid, get a degree in the Arts, and then move into theater then hopefully the movies. There was no way she was about to allow Shaun's tantrums interfere with what she had come to do. Déjà would have to just get herself together A.S.A.P and the only way that would happen, Jamie decided, was to take it to the hood. Jamie walked into the room pass Déjà. She stopped short then swung her body around while lifting her hand causing it to connect so hard with Déjà's face that Déjà's body fell back and onto her ass. Nick jumped forward grabbing Jamie by the neck.

"You stupid bitch why the fuck did you do that," Nick yelled into Jamie's ear as her hold became tighter. "Let her go Nick," Déjà moaned from her seated position. Jamie smiled grateful to see that her Ma'dam had pulled through. There was nothing wrong with taking things to the hood whenever the occasion arose.

Chapter 12

Déjà shook her head as Nick helped her off the ground. Looking directly at Jamie, Déjà stepped to her face to face. "Wipe that smile off your lips bitch. I understand why you put your hands on me, however never ever, do that shit again." More ghetto-fied then ever Déjà grilled Jamie for several seconds, causing Jamie to lower her eyes out of respect. "Yes ma'dam. I just thought..." Jamie tried to explain. "I know what you thought, but did I make myself clear?" "Yes."

Déjà shooed Jamie over to the side. She noticed Sergeant Wilcox still lying motionless in the center of the room; she barked her orders as though this type of situation happened every day. "Nick! Jheri! Come over here and get this sorry ass nigga out of here. Put his ass in the attic and make sure you make him as comfortable as possible, he'll probably be up there for a while. Renee get Shaun dressed and take her down to my office! The rest of you ladies get your pretty little asses back to work!" Then she walked out without a second glance. Angie frowned at that request. How the fuck can she go back into business mode when shit just hit the fan? Nicole and Jamie looked at each other as if to say, "is this woman for real?"

Although life at Butterflies had been rudely interrupted, it would be business as usual. She noticed her client heading in her direction. "Oh shit," Nicole whispered into the air as she quickly closed Shaun's door behind her. "Hey sweet daddy where are

87

you going? We aren't finished yet." "What was all that screaming about baby?" Short, stocky and handsome was nowhere near a good description for C.O Miller. 5ft 5 inches tall, with the complexion of hot coco, short curly black hair with long sideburns that crowned his oval shaped face. He had cat like eyes and delicious full lips that he always kept moisturized with his tongue. Nicole always told him that it was a sin to be that fine. When he had first crossed the threshold of Ma'dam Déjà's establishment, Nicole felt like she had died and gone to heaven. He roamed the living room viewing the goods Déjà had to offer with grace. His inspection was thorough and with great thought, carefully sizing up all of the ladies. Nicole had been the last one to come under his examination and when C.O. Miller choose her as his date for the evening, she felt the daggers being thrown at her back as she nonchalantly held his hand and escorted him up the stairs.

Once they reached the second level of the house, Nicole jumped at the opportunity. She pulled him close to her, stood on her tippy toes, because like Miller she was short, only 5ft 2 inches tall. Nicole nibbled, licked and caressed his lips. Passion had escaped her mouth as she kissed him tenderly, while her hands followed the curves of his body. His response and awareness was heartfelt. Without thinking about it he pushed her into him, giving her a feel of his erection. Pressed against him, she felt his manhood outlining his linen pants and hitting the frame of her coochie. Without delay, Nicole's juices began to seep through her panties. Not being able to wait one minute longer, Nicole pulled C.O. Miller towards her bedroom.

"Hey baby girl, what was that all about out there in the hallway," Miller asked her after closing the door behind him. "Honestly I couldn't help myself. From the minute you walked through the door I wanted to wrap my legs around your waist while you pounded into all of this," Nicole said while pointing towards her kitty with one hand as she released the belt from her silk robe with the other. Nicole exposed her precious diamond shaped pussy to him; she wanted him in the worse way. So bad that she would have been the one to pay the five hundred dollars she charged for an hour of pure satisfaction.

"So tell me Miller what do you desire," now removing her robe completely. "Damn girl I didn't know you got so much going on. What's your specialty?" Miller moved over by the window where a black leather love seat sat in a corner. With his back turned, C.O. Miller unbuttoned his shirt while his triceps swelled outwardly with each move. Nicole already had imagined climbing up over him, holding onto his bulging arms as she rode his manhood into another dimension. Although he wasn't very tall, Nicole could see that he was holding a big package. Nicole walked seductively towards him, and touched his shoulders gently; words couldn't begin to describe the heat that ran throughout her body. Miller turned around with a wicked smile on his face.

"So baby girl give me a brief description of your area of expertise." "Why don't I show you? We really don't have time for words unless you're talking dirty." Nicole slowly shoved him back towards the love seat, bringing him into a seated position.

Nicole stood before him caressing her perky nipples with her finger tips, causing them to become hard with passion. Miller's hand lowered into his pants as she enticed him with her sex appeal, she noticed how he stroked his boy toy so swiftly bringing his dick to its full size. Nicole was intoxicated by what she saw. Saliva began to build on her tongue when he released his driving force. She most definitely wanted to be on the driver's seat for this ride, but after getting a glimpse of him, she wouldn't mind riding as his passenger. He was that stacked! Being in control at all times had been one of her worse characteristic.

There were times when she knew she had to fall back and let someone else take control, but this wasn't going to be one of those times. Why change her technique now, when this fine ass creature was sitting directly in front of her handling his business. Up he moved his hand, hitting the tip of his manhood and down his hand glided over his shaft. It was the most sensual move Nicole had ever seen on a man. Nicole spread her legs apart allowing her nookie to expose freely. She inserted two of her fingers over the base of her tunnel while she gyrated her hips. Nicole was fully aware that C.O. Miller was watching her every move. He was not about to take his eyes off the prize

"Do you like that daddy," Nicole asked as she stroked her clit. "Yeah girl that shit looks good. Come over here and let me get a little taste of that." "Your wish is my command baby," Nicole responded. She lifted her fingers and placed them on Miller's

90

lips. He opened up and sucked her fingers hungrily. Nicole lowered herself onto his lap, straddling him while bringing both her thighs to meet his. Her eyes became misty from the need to feel him deeply within her. Gracefully, Nicole took Miller inch by inch, feeling him entering her. Half way down his shaft she bends forward to kiss his lips. Nicole wanted to taste her pussy too; she hoped to bring her excitement to its highest peak. Nicole continued to lower herself covering C.O. Miller's instrument completely with her tunnel. To Nicole's surprise she felt a sweet sensation near her G-spot. Slowly and seductively Nicole began to rotate her pelvic. She held onto his shoulders tightly, as he grabbed her waist and lifted himself up, so that he could be knee deep inside of her. It didn't take Nicole long to reach her first orgasm her - kitty just couldn't hold out any longer. His penetrating force caused her to reach places she had never reached before. Making the experience one she would not soon forget, C.O. Miller faced the challenge like a stallion.

He had really gotten into Nicole that first day. He liked the way she took him in. At no time did he feel like he was buying some ass; something he never had to do before because he had women. Sometimes more women than he could handle. He ended up at Butterflies out of curiosity. Butterflies had been the talk of the jail. C.O. to C.O. Déjà and her ladies had become an instant stimulator. Unable to believe the rumors C.O. Miller had decided to come take a look for himself. After seeing that the ladies were all classy, elegant and charming, he went along for the ride. Choosing Nicole had been out of curiosity too. It was the way that she kept her eyes glued to his. He liked a woman who knew what she wanted. She had made it clear from the very beginning that she wanted him. Shortly after their first date, C.O. Miller came back making his trips out to Déjà's establishment a weekly routine. But that was then.

"Listen, lets go back into my bedroom and finish what we started okay. One of the other girls was entertaining and things became a little too freaky." Nicole placed her hands on his chest, pushing him slowly back in the direction he had come from. "Besides I have something I want to show you." "Oh yeah what's that girl," Miller asked as he spanked her on the ass. "Well I can't show you out here." Nicole smiled wickedly moving over to the side of him. She began to walk towards her room, glancing over her shoulder she asked him. "Are you coming?" "No doubt baby, and this better be good." "You know that it is good, that's why you keep coming back." "You ain't never lie," Miller stated as they disappeared into her bedroom.

Jamie and Angie were not in the mood to go into their bedroom. Not once did they think that something like this could happen; they thought that they were safe from the lunatics of the world. They had heard stories of violence, rapes, and sometimes death within the profession, but those things happened to the streetwalkers, who sold their bodies on a street corner. They were the ones who risked everything for the Ol' mighty dollars. Every time they got into a tricks car they took the chance of never returning.

Butterflies, was supposed to be a safe heaven for women who worked under a watchful eye. Together they walked down the hall and into their domains, but before they closed the doors behind them they winked at each other. They had decided that once they completed their sessions they would sit down and have a long talk with their ma'dam. The screening process would have to change. They were not willing to work under dangerous conditions.

Chapter 13

Meanwhile downstairs on the main floor, Déjà stormed into her office finding Destiny comfortably sitting with her feet propped up on her desk. The sight of Destiny violating her space made her blood boil. Not only did she not come to the aid of one of her sista's she sat there as though she owned the fuckin place. Déjà got the impression that she was trying to out shine her and the others. "Get your feet off my desk," Déjà shouted as she rounded the desk quickly and snatched the chair from under her.

"How dare you!" "I'm sorry Déjà." "Don't be sorry Destiny, be careful," Déjà snapped at Destiny with venom in her voice. "Shaun freaked out and striked the Sergeant with a metal object," Destiny replied before she walked over by the cameras. "Do me a favor and rewind the tape," Déjà said as she sat back on her black swivel chair because she needed to take a look at the monitors to see what really happened.

Destiny complied with Déjà's request, but didn't appreciate how she was ordering her around as though she was beneath her. If Destiny didn't know any better, she would have thought that Déjà considered herself to be too good. Déjà, however wasn't about to accept that type of behavior or anything else in that nature. Violence came in the worse forms and at the worse times - shit happens. If she had been the one who had been running Butterflies, she would have just taken care of the situation without so much drama. Better yet, she probably

95

would have disposed of Sergeant Wilcox's body. Fuck it, if he was still alive he wasn't going to go away quietly if he recovered.

Unfortunately that was not what Déjà had in mind. Déjà's plan probably was to nurse him back to health and convince him that it was just a misunderstanding on Shaun's part. Destiny was sure of this. Déjà wasn't the ghetto type who carried the street mentality and that was without a doubt going to be her downfall. Desperate times caused for desperate measures. After rewinding the tape, Destiny went over to the door and opened it to find Shaun and Renee standing on the other side looking twisted. Shaun was shaking uncontrollably with tears pouring down her face, causing her make-up ran down the side of her cheeks. Her hair was a mess and still wet from her shower Renee was looking just as upset. Destiny couldn't help but to wonder what was running through her mind. Quietly she turned around, walked back over to the panel, and waited for them to come in and take their places around Déjà's desk. Renee stared at Destiny; she could feel Destiny's negativity. Her cold heartless ways didn't go unnoticed.

"Shaun are you alright," Déjà asked in a low tone. She didn't want to upset her anymore than she already was. Shaun shook her head, letting Déjà know that she was alright. Although Shaun had reacted the way that she did, she knew that what she had done was going to cause chaos amongst the other ladies. Of course Déjà was going to be the one to pay the highest price because it was her place and rep that was on the line. However this was not fair to the others. Everything they had worked so hard for, would now go down the drain. They weren't going to take that lightly and let's not forget how easily she could be returned to Albion.

"Shaun please sit down." Renee pointed towards a lounge chair. "Nah I'm good," Shaun stated angrily. "Ma'dam," Renee called on Déjà for some support. "Shaun listen I realize that you are very upset but I need you to calm down so that we can figure out what were going to do next." "Why don't you just cut all the bullshit out Déjà? You know damn well what's going to happen next. My ass is going back to the P-nile for assault on an officer." "It's not that deep Shaun," Renee now spoke out of pocket. "Not that deep? What? Are you really feeding into this lifestyle? You know damn well that Sergeant Wilcox is not going to walk away without a fight. I already have one state bid under my belt and he knows that if word got out that he was fraternizing with the forbidden fruit, he could lose his job along with his pension. He would never allow me to get away with that no matter how good the pussy is."

Renee had to think about that. Since she had gotten caught up with the lifestyle Déjà had given her she had forgotten where she had come from. They were not dealing with a chump (Vic), so coupled with the fact that these men that crossed the line everyday for a few minutes of pleasure had plenty to lose, not only did they have families and friends that they had to answer to, if ever caught having an extra marital affair, they would have a community of law enforcers looking down on them. In a small town such as Albion N.Y., these types of acts were done discreetly, not in the open with a bunch of call girls who were ex-convicts.

"Look, there is no need to get crazy. We have to maintain in order to work this out," Déjà spoke to Renee. "Play the tape Destiny," again Déjà spoke with venom in her voice. It was the way that Destiny stood close by with a smirk on her face that caused her to treat her in such an ill manner.

Nick opened the door to Shaun's bedroom and quietly stuck her head out to look down the hall. When she realized that the coast was clear, she rushed over to the attic door and unlocked it with a key. She hurried back to where Jheri had already dragged the body halfway into the hallway. "Chill nigga let me get his legs," Nick whispered already out of breath. "Hurry your ass up!" Together they carried the Sergeant up the stairs. "Where the fuck are we going to put him," Jheri asked Nick. "I don't know maybe we can put his ass over here by this corner," Nick hollered. "This nigga is heavy." With Sergeant Wilcox still out for the count, Jheri ran around the attic gathering old blankets, sheets, and old clothing left over from previous owners. She spread them out and with Nick's help, placed Sergeant Wilcox's body on top.

"Now what," Jheri questioned as she looked down at the Sergeant. "I'm not sure. Déjà will figure it out." "You think? You know damn well that Déjà ain't into no shit like this. Remember she is one of them. How the fuck is she going to explain this to the po-po?" "It's like I said she'll figure it out." Nick didn't believe that last statement herself. She knew Déjà better than most and Jheri was right when she said that Déjà wasn't into anything like this.

Clearly the Department of Corrections would report the Sergeant missing; his disappearance would leak out among the family and neighbors resulting with the authorities getting involved. Once an investigation was in full force, someone was bond to mention the Ma'dam C.O. and her ladies of the night. Butterflies and everyone involved would be in Jeopardy. Nick knew that Déjà wasn't equipped to handle such a situation. So she had no choice but to come up with a plan of her own.

Although Nick was rarely in street mode, nowadays the streets were still in her blood, so destruction wasn't too far behind. Especially when it came to someone she was feeling. "Yo what's up with you man, I see that look in your eyes. I know you ain't trying to scheme?" "Nah man I'm good." Nick smiled. "Alright then let's head downstairs." Jheri suddenly turned around and walked down the steps. Nick stood behind for a few seconds, lowered her head and said a silent prayer, "God help me."

She knew that what she was about to do if caught could cause them a lifetime behind the walls of hell. Albion wouldn't even be an option; it was straight to Bedford Hills for her if she didn't come up with a solid plan.

Chapter 14

All four women watched the tape attentively. When it had finally come to its end, no one said a word. Destiny watched Renee and Shaun closely, while Renee and Shaun watched Déjà. Laid back in her seat, Déjà thought about what she had just witnessed. Shaun exited the bathroom completely nude, rubbing a towel over her head. Looking up as she entered the room, she noticed Sergeant Wilcox sitting on her ottoman. Shaun began speaking smoothly at first asking the Sergeant what he was still doing there. His response was one that Shaun was not expecting. He expressed his disapproval of her behavior. Shaun became offended, then asked him to leave. She quickly turned towards the hidden camera to signal Destiny, who Shaun knew was watching, by winking. Sergeant Wilcox noticed her move before he stood up. Then before she knew what was happening, he reached out to grab her by the arm. Shaun pulled back and ran towards the head of her bed. She lifted her mattress slightly and removed a Chinese black jack. She jerked it open, and then began to swing wildly.

The fear that came across Shaun's face froze Déjà because she had recognized it so many times before. No one in that room could relate to that type of fear like she could. Flash backs of her ex-husband beating her ass came into play as she continued to observe Shaun's desperate attempt to protect herself. When one of the blows connected directly onto the Sergeant's head he went down. Blood ran down the side of his face and his eyes rolled back. Déjà then heard the knock at the door. If only she would have gotten up there a few seconds earlier, none of this would have happened.

If only Destiny would have pressed the emergency button on the panel, all of the other ladies would have been alerted that someone was in trouble. That alone was not sitting right with her. But it was too late for should've, would've, could've. The tape recordings had upset Déjà so much that now she sat in her office amongst her ladies at a loss for words. What could she possibly say or do to fix the situation at hand. What could she say to ease Shaun's mind? Suddenly Déjà searched deep down. The reality of it all is that if she would have been put out there the way that Shaun was, she would have done the very same thing. Déjà was a little disappointed in herself; if she wouldn't have been so hungry for Nick and all the good loving she gave her, she would have been at Butterflies handling her business instead of in New York City fucking her brains out in the middle of the street. Disappointments, plus regrets, would have to be put on the back burner for now.

Though the feeling was there digging deep into her soul, Déjà had to remember what Ms. Garcia had instilled in her at the shelter. That it was just a feeling and it would pass. Everything that happens in life had to be taken as a lesson, an opportunity to show your strengths. Weakness would only be the obstacle to hold up her progress. She had come a long way from those days. The woman that she was today was not supposed to be surprised at all by what had taken place upstairs in Shaun's

102

bedroom. Those incidents were bound to happen, especially in this type of business.

Déjà stood up and paced the small space that stood between her and the others, thinking of her next move. "The outcome of Sergeant Wilcox's accident will only bring negative publicity," Déjà thought. Not only will there be a public broadcast, A.P.B out on him, she had to figure out a way of protecting other gentlemen callers. Deja had given her word to them, promising to never divulge their names no matter what the circumstances. Most of the men that arrived at Déjà's door step had been referred to her by other clients; either by word of mouth, or casual invitations. It will be a difficult task, but one she was sure she could handle. Glancing at her diamond Rolex watch, Déjà realized that the sun would be going down soon, bringing into closure phase one of her operation and the opening of another. Friday nights, Déjà had learned from working with so many men at the Facility that these evenings were always the busiest. After working 7 to 16 hour shifts at a Correctional Facility, the C.O.s looked forward to a night of leisure. Butterflies would transform into a place where they found relaxation, privacy and plenty of entertainment. Business would go on as usual. Déjà wasn't about to shut it down because there was money to be made! Once the evening was over with, she would decide what to do next.

Nick stood by the French doors that lead out onto the grounds. All the gentlemen who remained in the house completed their sessions and had finally departed. "There goes another satisfied customer," Nick said while watching them climb into their SUV's. "Yeah I can see that them chumps had really gotten their shit off. I wouldn't mind getting a little head right about now," Jheri said as she walked up on Nick. "I bet," Nick responded wickedly. "I know your ass ain't saying nothing slick, not with the way you walked up in here this afternoon." "Mind your business Jheri." "You ain't got no business son. Your business is out there nigga." "Whatever," Nick smiled as she thought about how just a few hours ago Déjà was bent down at the knee's giving a nigga something to think about! "Yo on a serious tip you better be easy." "Why?" "Cause Nick, you getting yourself all caught in a feeling. Mind you, you know that Déjà be turning tricks too."

Nick didn't even wait for Jheri to continue on in her down talking of Déjà. She immediately grabbed Jheri by the throat, pinning her up against one of the glass doors. "Don't even try to disrespect me kid." "Yo chill Nick what the fuck is wrong with you?" "I'm a show you what the fuck is wrong with me." Nick placed her other hand on Jheri's throat and began to squeeze. She knew that what Jheri was saying about Déjà was true. Déjà turned more tricks than the average hoe, but Nick didn't want to see it for what it really was. That old hustler saying came to her as she tried to take Jheri's last breath. You can never make a hoe into a housewife but you can make a housewife into a hoe. Those words would haunt her for as long as she held these feelings for the Ma'dam C.O.

"Oh shit," Destiny hollered bringing Déjà out of her trance. "What Destiny?" "Nick is in the foyer choking the shit out of Jheri. Look," Destiny now pointing at one of the monitors, laughing. "What the hell is so funny? You've been acting strange all fucking day. What's really good," Déjà now confronted Destiny. "I know you ain't using no profanity Ms. Ma'dam?" "Don't get cocky bitch. I ain't in the mood for your bullshit. Get your ass out my fucking office," Déjà snapped. Destiny walked towards the door then turned back to look at Renee. "Let's get the fuck out of here, Nene." "I'll be right there. Go to your room and wait for me." Renee looked from Destiny to Déjà.

Déjà was about to leave her office to check out what Nick's confrontation with Jheri was all about. But before she was able to leave Renee stopped her. "Ma'dam you know that if Destiny leaves, then I will have to leave too. We came in this together." "Then do what you have to do. But remember you will be giving up much more than just a home, you will be giving up your dream of getting an education. What is it Renee, do you want to go back to the streets and do you what you were doing before you went to prison?" "But." "There are no buts, Think about what you say before you say it. Renee, you have a lot to lose."

Renee lowered her eyes then sat back down and cradled Shaun in her arms. Déjà looked on with pride. These young ladies, that filled her home with nothing but determination to change their futures, reminded her of the days when she

105

attended the academy. Yeah she was determined to leave her abusive husband and make a life for herself and the kids, however her alter ego was determined to become a Ma'dam. So she understood Renee's turmoil. The streets were calling out to her. Some women were stronger than others and Déjà hoped that Renee was one of the stronger ones. Because there was no doubt in her mind that Destiny was the weaker of the two.

"I'll be right back. You ladies take a minute and get your thoughts together. We have a big night ahead of us. We are going to masquerade party." Déjà turned on her heels and left them alone.

Chapter 15

In the hallway, Déjà took a deep breath. She felt as though she was about to have an anxiety attack. Not only did she have to come up with a solution to Shaun's problem, now she had to figure out what the hell was wrong with Nick. It had to be something serious because that type of behavior was totally unacceptable. Nick had a high tolerance for bullshit, so she must have been really pissed off to reach out and touch Jheri. Déjà overheard Nick threaten Jheri, and had decided to put an end to whatever was going on between them before something else happened.

Spontaneously Déjà rushed towards them. Before she was able to make it down the long hallway Nick's words stopped her. "Stop right there Déjà. Take your ass back to your office!"

Déjà remained speechless. At first she was shocked that Nick would dare speak to her in that tone. When that feeling passed, Nick reminded her at that moment why she desired Nick so much, since the very first day she laid eyes on her - it was her strong demeanor.

It was the way that Nick held her ground; the way that she played her role, with so much passion. Déjà found that to be a great asset. Nick had no idea how powerful she was when it came to her. Naturally Déjà wouldn't show it for many different reasons. The main one being that she wasn't gay and wouldn't know how to live her life as a lesbian if she had decided to come out of the closet. Nick had been her first experience and as far as she was concerned she would be her last. Nick's love making was so potent that at times she did think about giving up her Ma'dams' status and settling in with her as her full time lover.

However, the reality would shift those thoughts in another direction because how would her daughters feel if they knew that their mother was shacking up with another woman? Even though they were still too young to understand the fundamental laws of nature, they did know that boys loved girls and vice versa; but that was as far as their little minds went on that subject. Their foundation could possibly be shattered if she confused them by trying to live a normal life with Nick. It was too risky. Her job as a mother was to instill morals, values, and beliefs; to protect her daughters from a society that already judged them, if for nothing else for the color of their skin. They didn't need to be looked on as the lesbian's daughters as well. Plus what in the world would they call Nick, papa, mama, auntie, uncle ... Nadiva already thought that Nick was a man. If she allowed herself to run with the feeling, her daughters would eventually find out the truth and maybe disapprove of Nick's lifestyle, causing her to have conflicts with them. Déjà wasn't prepared for that because she had other things she needed to concentrate on.

"Nick I don't know if you realized this, but I'm the only one who can bark orders around here! Now take your hands off of Jheri and be easy! I have too much shit to deal with right now and I don't need you to add to it," Déjà stood firmly. Nick's body

108

began to tremble. She was vexed, but before Nick released Jheri she asked her if she had understood her request to never disrespect her by talking shit about Déjà. Jheri was way out of line with the remark she made and Nick wanted to make her point clear. Jheri examined her neck and collarbone, then spoke directly to Déjà in a horse voice, "If you need me I'll be downstairs in the lounge."

Alone now Déjà and Nick faced each other. "What the hell was that all about Nick?" Déjà crossed her arms over her chest. "Don't worry about it." "What do you mean don't worry about it!" "Like I said don't worry about it. You have other things to deal with, right," Nick stated. "Yes I do, however one thing doesn't have to do with the other. You know you are dead ass wrong by trying to throw that up in my face!" "Whatever Ma'dam." "Yeah whatever Nick. Why are you playing yourself?"

Déjà walked the long hallway towards her. There was one thing Nick never did in the past six months since their introduction and that was to disrespect her. They never once argued over anything. So for Nick to speak to her in such a demanding tone was new to her. "What's going on with you," Déjà leaned in now placing her face close to Nick's. "You." "Me?" "Yeah, when are you going to stop all of this shit? When we first got together you told me that you just wanted to open up shop, sell other people's property and reap the benefits." "Well isn't that what I'm doing," Déjà whispered while stroking Nick's face. "That and much more, Déjà." "Why don't you just get to the point baby." "Never mind. What the fuck are you going to do about your little situation," Nick asked changing the subject and pointing toward the attic.

"I have no idea. There is so much to consider. Hopefully once he comes to I'll convince him to not press charges. I was on my way up there now." Déjà's eyes roamed a little before she looked at Nick again. "Do you want me to go with you?" "Nah it's best if I go alone. I don't want him freaking out or anything." "Listen I apologize for talking to you the way that I did," Nick expressed her regret hoping to clear the air between them. "It's alright we are all under a lot of pressure, but we have to work together at this point." Déjà started to become emotional. "I feel you girl. Go do what you got to do." Nick walked around Déjà, then commenced to walk down the hall toward the living room.

"Alright baby," the Ma'dam C.O. whispered softly. At that very moment Déjà felt as though she was going to break down. Her feelings for Nick were so strong. She wondered how she had allowed herself to fall in love with her. She also wondered how or when it even happened. Control was a big factor in Déjà's life, but lately she had very little of that when it came to her emotions.

Déjà quickly wiped some tears away. She inhaled deeply and got a whiff of Nick's cologne. "Damn she smells so good." Suddenly she could feel something slippery between her thighs. Her desire for Nick came at her once again, with a little discretion she wiggled her legs together. It was so difficult for her to hold her composure because her coochie had a mind of its own. "Control Déjà, Control," she said to herself before she walked towards the attic.

Chapter 16

In the attic, Déjà walked quietly towards Sergeant Wilcox, bent down next to him and checked his pulse with caution. It was there, however very weak. Though life at Butterflies had taken a turn for the worse, Déjà had to maintain a sense of stability. Her future as well as the future of her girls, Navida and Brianna, was at stake. Her mind was going a thousand miles a minute, with thoughts of what she should do about Shaun.

Déjà began to think that she was a failure, of course through no fault of her own. Déjà had taken the necessary steps to ensure everyone's safety by checking the Sergeant's background as well as his state of mind. Coming up short on the security tip brought her outlook on her abilities at an all time low. How could she overlook his lack of confidence? Déjà never noticed anything strange during his sessions with Shaun. The only thing that came to mind now that she thought about it, was that he refused to date any of the other girls.

If Shaun was out attending her own personal business, Sergeant Wilcox would leave then return when she was available. Déjà on many occasions had tried to accommodate him by even offering herself. But his answer was always the same, "No thank you."

Covering his body with an old blanket, Déjà noticed that his breathing was shallow. Afraid that he would die, Déjà hurried back down the steps in search of Nick. Turning the corner quickly Déjà bumped into Destiny, who was, Déjà guessed,

113

going to her bedroom? "Destiny have you seen Nick?" "Nah she's probably in the lounge. Why?" "There is something wrong with Sergeant Wilcox, he isn't breathing right and his pulse is getting weaker by the minute. I don't know what the hell to do." Déjà was losing control. She stared at Destiny who stood directly in front of her with a smirk on her face.

"Destiny I told you this shit wasn't funny, fix your face." "Ha, I never thought that I would see this day." "What do you mean?" "You know the day that I would actually see you sweat. Déjà you walk around here with your grandiose attitude as though shit can't happen to you. Welcome to the real world!" "Destiny what the hell are you talking about, you ungrateful little bitch? How fucking dare you try to evaluate me? If it wasn't for me your ass would still be in the streets pick pocketing innocent people out of their hard earned money." "Probably so, but at least the money I made stayed in my mutherfuckin pocket. I can't believe that I allowed myself to be talked into selling my ass for someone else."

Destiny lit a cigarette as she glared at Déjà with an evil eye. "Well sweetie, for your information that was a choice you made. You could have gone about your business. You wasn't doing me no favors." "True that, but it was really hard to tell Nick no. That bitch is so smooth; she makes a motherfucker cream instantly with just the sound of her voice."

Destiny had finally crossed the line, and was quite proud of herself just by the look on Déjà's face; she sensed that she had hit a nerve. "It's funny that you say that Destiny, that's exactly the reason why I hired her to recruit your sorry ass." Déjà arched her back with integrity refusing to allow Destiny's remark to affect her. She continued, she wasn't about to let Destiny have the last word, "If the sound of her voice can make you cream, imagine what the rest of her could do to you. Unfortunately you'll never get that far." "How do you know for sure that I haven't Ms. I-got- the- world-by-the-balls?" "Well, it doesn't matter if you have or not. The bottom line is that you signed on to do what you do best. Lying on your back as well as kneeling down at the waist, your moves have proven to be profitable. Thank you for providing your services to my and I repeat MY establishment. I estimate that if I was to let you go right now I can still live quite nicely off the money you made." "It's interesting that you say that ma'dam. Did it ever occur to you that maybe the money I made will contribute to your bail? You know for a fact that Sergeant Wilcox is going to have your ass. So I suggest you use that money to pay for your defense." Destiny's smile ran right through Déjà. "So you see ma'dam you don't have to let me go. I'm leaving. Good luck!"

Destiny walked pass Déjà with her head elevated whispering, "Bitch," under breath. Once she arrived at the entrance to her bedroom door. She looked back and noticed Déjà standing at the far end of the hallway, stuck on stupid. Entering her bedroom she found Renee and Shaun waiting for her. She closed the door behind her, while removing her 3"inch Gucci stilettos, then sat on a plush leather trunk that rested at the end of her king size bed, anxious to get as far away as she could from Butterflies she spoke firmly at Renee, "So did you decide what it is you're going to do?" "Destiny listen," Renee responded standing fully erect. "You know that if you leave I'm out too!" "So what are you waiting for, go pack your shit. By the time you're done I'll be ready." Destiny stood up, walked over to the walk-in closet and removed a duffle bag from the top shelf. Immediately she began to pack.

Shaun knew in her heart of hearts that she didn't want to live her life as a prostitute. She thought about the choices she had made and realized that she had been turned out to the lifestyle out of ignorance. She was looking for someone to fill a void. Her parents never noticed how lonely she had been throughout the years. They thought that material things would compensate for their lack of attention. Being lonely was far worse than anything she had experienced in her short existence. Soon she would be twenty four years old, and there definitely had to be more to life than this. She wanted out. This was her one and only chance to escape all of the trials and tribulations this business had to offer.

Shaun thought about the man who laid dying in the attic and prison was not an option for her. Her first go around was a skid bid, being at the wrong place at the wrong time. Murder in the first degree meant a lifetime at Bedford Hills Correctional Facility. No way was she going back. Images of Bedford alone caused her to jump up and say, "I'm leaving too!" Destiny stopped packing and looked at her. Not sure she had heard Shaun correctly, Destiny asked her. "What did you just say?" "I said I'm leaving too." "Oh yeah, what are you going to do about

116

your little problem missy?" "It ain't my fucking problem, its Déjà's." Shaun was aware that her last statement sounded grimy, but said it anyway. "To leave Déjà holding the bag would be fucked up. But better her than you right," Destiny questioned. "Des let's keep it real, what the fuck am I suppose to do? Just sit here and wait for an investigation to begin. You know these fucking crackers are going to start looking for him soon." "Unless." Destiny said as an afterthought. "Unless what?" "Unless we take him with us?" Destiny now kneeled down in front of Shaun. "I know you're kidding right," Shaun stared deeply into Destiny's eyes. "Hell no I'm not kidding. Do you really think that Déjà is going to take the fall and not implicate you? The bitch ain't got one loyal hair on her head Shaun. She only thinks about herself, we have to take matters into our own hands." "You think?" Not sure if she could totally agree with Destiny about Déjà being selfish because Déjà had always seemed to take her feelings into consideration.

Shit was getting real complicated. It never dawned on Shaun that Déjà would be put in a position to expose her. Destiny did have more to say about resolving the problem. Déjà had been acting as though she had shit under control, but the reality was that she didn't. Besides if push comes to shove, she wouldn't give up her life for hers. Shaun felt the tears rolling down her face and confusion began to invade her thoughts. If in fact Destiny was willing to help her, she would jump at the chance. There was one remaining factor though ... Sergeant Wilcox was still alive.

117

Chapter 17

C.O. Miller, Steward and Collins all drove away pleased with the treatment they had received at Butterflies. Each looked forward to their next visit which would be this evening. The masquerade party was going to be a big event that no one in their right mind would miss. As the three officers went their separate ways C.O. Miller felt like there was something missing, but he couldn't quite put his finger on it.

Nevertheless, there was a nagging feeling at the pit of his stomach. He searched through his memory bank of clues, but nothing came to mind. Pulling over by the side of the road, he stepped out onto the pavement then, searched his pockets. With his wallet in one hand and condoms in the other, it hit him like a ton of bricks, it was the Sergeant. He hadn't recalled seeing the Sergeant again once he went into the bedroom with Shaun. Miller remembered clearly seeing him being escorted upstairs, but he didn't see him leave the premises. He laughed it off at first because he knew Sergeant Wilcox couldn't get enough of Shaun.

Everyone who participated in the sex for hire trade knew that the Sergeant was strung out on the pussy. There was talk among the gentlemen about how he had started behaving extremely over protective of Déjà and her ladies. His obsession had become much more than just satisfying his appetite. Running out of work when his shift was over; swapping days, hours, and even minutes just to be with Shaun. It seemed kind of sick now that he thought about it. Miller had chucked it off back then as just another brother getting his freak on. Now, he thought twice about it. Jumping back into his SUV, Miller made a complete U-Turn and then headed back towards Butterflies.

Déjà reached the bottom of the steps with the weight of the world on her shoulders. Her emotions were running wild and the last thing she needed at this point in her life was a dying man in her attic. Walking over to where Nick sat drinking a tall glass of cognac, she slowly spread Nick's legs and bent down before her, while placing her head on Nick's thigh. They remained quiet for a few seconds. All that was heard through out the lounge was their breathing and Nick taking slow sips from her glass from time to time. Nick was the first one to speak, "Is everything alright upstairs?" "Baby I think the Sergeant is dying. His breathing is abnormal and I'm afraid to call the ambulance." "You can't do that baby girl. Once the authorities get wind of what's been going on in here you can end up not only losing everything, but going to jail." "Yeah I know, so what am I going to do?" Déjà now lifted her head to look into Nick's eyes. "Don't worry baby. Your knight in shining Armor is right here." Nick pulled Déjà towards her and planted a deep passionate kiss on her lips. Breathless, Déjà asked Nick, "What do you have planned baby? We have to do something soon. The party is in a few hours."

Nick placed her glass on one of the tables off to the side of her. "Once it starts getting dark we are going up to get him. We will place him in his car and drive him someplace where hopefully

120

someone will find him and get him the medical attention he needs." "Isn't that risky? How are we going to get him out of the house without anyone noticing," Déjà asked with fear in her voice. "Girl let me take care of all the details. You just follow my lead." Nick placed a hand on the tip of Déjà's breast stroking her nipple in full circles.

Taking in a deep breath from the touch, Déjà responded, "I trust you. I know that you wouldn't let anything happen to me." Déjà now began to unbutton her silk blouse exposing full breasts under a Victoria's Secret push-up bra. Déjà placed Nicks hand on her delicate skin. A rush of electricity ran throughout her body like a powerhouse. There was no doubt in her mind, that although she knew there would be consequences from this relationship, this is where she belonged. Déjà was not about to keep fighting the demons that stood in the way of her happiness. She was going to surrender to Nick fully and completely.

After they took care of their little situation, she would make the announcement in front of the others. Nick deserved to be acknowledged as her lover; there would be no more creeping around between them. Déjà reached for Nick's jeans, pulled her zipper down slowly to find what her pussy craved, Nick's toy. Placing her mouth on the tip, she licked the head seductively causing wetness between her legs instantly. Lubricating the toy fully with her mouth, Déjà stood up, then turned around giving Nick a full view of her ass as she lifted her skirt.

"Damn girl come show daddy how much you love her.". Déjà spread her legs, then lowered herself onto Nick's 10" dildo. "Show me girl". Nick murmured in her ear as she held onto Déjà's pelvic bones and glided her movements against her own.

Meanwhile upstairs in Destiny's room Renee and Shaun remained quiet while Destiny described word for word her plan. Her plan of action sounded so surreal that Shaun's fears of going back to prison crept up again. On the other hand Renee's attitude was one of full confidence. She believed that Destiny's plan would work. Shaun could see why the two made a perfect pair. They had more then selling coochie in common; Destiny and Renee were wicked. Where one would plan some outrageous scheme, the other would be quick to act it out without thinking twice about the consequences, Destiny used Renee's ride or die attitude to her advantage. Shaun didn't trust either one of them, but under the circumstances she didn't have much of a choice. It was either go along with them on their crazy scheme, or stay at Butterflies and face the chance of being sort out by everyone in Orleans County.

Shaun had decided to take a risk on Renee and Destiny. What would be the worst thing that could happen? She could get away with it. That was something to think about. "O.K. then, Shaun did you hear what I just said?" "Yeah!" "Alright then girls let's get this show on the road. We can make it back to the city before sun break if we move out now." Destiny grabbed her duffel bag, which she had stuffed with everything she thought

122

she would need for the trip. Little did they know that one flight up from where they were discussing their plan to remove Sergeant Wilcox from the premises, Sergeant Wilcox had taken his last breath.

Chapter 18

C.O. Eric Miller parked his SUV by the side of the road, looked out of the driver's side window and saw Butterflies in full view. The sun was beginning to set and the temperature was changing quickly, shivering from the cold chill that spread across the town of Albion, N.Y. Eric jumped out of his ride zipped up his leather jacket, then flipped the collar up to cover his neck. Before Eric began to walk towards the woods, he said a silent pray. He found a small path that would lead him to the two story stature undetected.

When he finally made the short walk towards the house, he came upon a set of bay windows. Eric peeked in and saw Jamie and Angie enter the front parlor with their hands full of crystal glasses, gently placing them on the bar, where in a few hours gentlemen of leisure would be drinking their sorrows away. It was a pretty sight. Jamie was already dressed in her costume wearing a custom made black petty coat skirt and matching full figure bustier with high thigh patent leather boots. Jamie resembled a dungeon master, who gentlemen turned to, to fulfill their fantasies of becoming slaves. If only for a few hours these women who called themselves dominatrix would become the force behind the weak minded men who would request some of the weirdest acts imaginable. Angie, who had left the living room while Jamie continued to set up the bar, was still wearing her silk bathrobe.

C.O. Miller noticed how the lights were turned down low, giving the candles that flickered in the background a soft, but yet mysterious look. This had given him a strange feeling. He had received his invitation personally from Nicole and he most definitely had plans of attending the party. Nevertheless his instincts told him that he was about to embark on something much more. Next he noticed Nicole walking into the room. She too had been dressed for the big event wearing a full body leather cat suit, knee high boots and a silver belt wrapped around her small waist, resembling Halley Berry in "Cat Woman."

Eric couldn't help himself when he thought back to how dynamic Nicole was in the bedroom, with her million and one positions. He could see why she would pick that particular costume because it matched her personality to the fullest. Hot and slick in her demeanor, Nicole went over to the bar, poured herself a drink, then began to converse with Jamie, who was complaining about how the others were nowhere to be found.

"It's funny how when it's time to do some work around here these bitches disappear." "Who you talking about girl," Nicole asked while taking small sips of what looked to be Alize. "Renee, Shaun and Destiny!" "Oh well, I haven't seen them since … you know," Nicole stated as if someone could hear their conversation. "Yeah I know, Nicole I've been thinking," Jamie paused for a second, spun around then headed towards the French doors that separated the living room from the foyer.

She peeked out, then looked from side to side, wanting to make sure that no one was headed into the living room. Then she closed the doors, walking back towards Nicole who now moved away from the bar. She got right up on her and continued. "What's up Jamie you acting all nervous and shit, what's on your mind?" "I've been thinking about leaving." "Leaving! Where the fuck do you think you're going?" "SHHHH chill girl, you going to blow up my spot. I'm thinking about going back to the city where else?" "To do what Jamie?" Nicole backed up a little and placed her hand on her waist. With her neck in motion Nicole looked Jamie up and down.

"Not to change the subject or anything Jamie but you sure are looking good in that outfit." Nicole wasn't stressing Jamie's outburst. It was pointless because Jamie was one of those types that changed her mind from one minute to the next. "Stop playing Nicky." "Umm I love it when you call me that. You know how to press my buttons," Nicole responded while licking her lips. It had been no secret to Jamie that Nicole was bisexual, she had made it a point of letting everyone know that she liked to lick French buttons on occasion. Jamie noticed Nicole size her up when they first met; she had a freaky side to her, and for a dollar she would do just about anything. However, she never really thought twice about freaking off with another chick to satisfy her own needs.

Jamie had never broken the number one rule in the sex industry, which was never to give up the goodies without getting paid. Nicole's inspection of her began to make her feel uncomfortable. Heat began to creep up over the side of her neck, causing her face to become flushed. Turning away from Nicole to break the connection, Jamie felt her most private parts become sensitive. For months now Jamie had faked her way around the bedroom. It had been a long time since she had reached the highest point of sexual excitement with anyone. Even when she was alone, orgasms were very hard to come by because her days had been filled with pleasing everyone else. When free to do of her own thing she was too exhausted.

Jamie walked back over to the bar and poured herself a double shot of Brandy. She threw her head back and in one huge gulp the liquid substance had disappeared, burning her throat yet it didn't distract her thoughts of the heat that was ablaze between her legs. Looking over the rim of her glass Jamie watched Nicole's reflection bounce off the full length mirrors that surrounded the room. From behind Nicole fit perfectly in her cat suit; her ass was firm, her waist small and the small of her back even and smooth, free from any bulges or extra fat. Her hour glass shape reminded Jamie of the old fashion Pepsi cola bottles her grandmother now used as penny holders.

Nicole, fully aware that she had caught Jamie's attention with her flirtatious ways, decided to give her a full rear-end view of what she was holding in her love box. Lowering herself forward from the waist, Nicole bent over to wipe away some carpet fibers from the tip of her boots, wiggling her ass a little along the way. Nicole exposed much more than her derrière as the material of her cat suit extended, exposing her pussy unfold in its crotch less bottoms. Freshly shaved and trimmed, Nicole's kitty smiled up at Jamie.

Before Jamie could make her next move, she noticed a glare by the side of the mirror. Choosing to ignore it, Jamie walked away from the bar once again. This time with nothing on her mind but the inferno that burned down below. Jamie headed for the one person standing in the room that could cool her down. Slowly pushing Nicole up against the wall, Jamie passionately began to kiss her. Fucking her mouth with every stroke of her tongue, Nicole began to whine against Jamie's leg. Nicole had no idea that Jamie was capable of showing such emotions, and she wasn't about to complain either. This was exactly what she wanted.

Feeling a little overpowered by Jamie, Nicole changed positions. Jamie was now the one who had her back against the wall. Bringing her thigh up against Jamie's crotch, Nicole began to move her leg up and down. She could feel the heat of Jamie's pussy cutting right through her leather suit. Lifting her skirt slightly, Jamie became bolder as Nicole fucked her. She grabbed a hold of Nicole's ass and pushed her in closer. Jamie's legs spread open widely, whining her coohie into Nicole's clit. Making contact she softly rubbed it against the cool leather material. With tongues entwined and in another state of mind, neither one of them noticed the man in the window.

C.O. Miller couldn't believe what he was witnessing. Nicole had told him once that she had never indulged with the other females in the house. Her lies disappointed him because he was really looking forward to a threesome with one of the other ladies, but C.O. Miller just never pushed the issue. Now after seeing Nicole for who she really was, Eric wished that he had demanded it of her. His dick was rock hard and in need of some deep penetration, so he lowered his zipper, releasing her manhood, then continued to watch the little ladies in action.

Jamie held on to Nicole's shoulders as she lowered then raised herself against her thigh. The friction was so overpowering that her loud moans penetrated through the walls. "SSHH baby. They're going to hear us." "UUMMM I can't help it. This shit feels so fuckin good." "Do your thing girl. I knew you had it in you," Nicole cheered her on as she pushed into Jamie's love box a little harder. Bringing Jamie up on her tippy toes, Nicole released her bustier with her teeth. Her breast stood so firm on her chest, that Nicole found no difficulty in inserting Jamie's nipple into her mouth, sucking on them carefully causing Jamie to reach her first orgasm.

"Come on baby give it to me." "Oh shit Nicky. I'm a cum baby!!" Pushing her leg into her deeper, unable to control her movements Jamie began to climb up the walls. Nicole also couldn't help herself when she placed her hand under Jamie's skirt. She spread Jamie's lips and finger fucked her. One, two, three and then finally the fourth finger slipped inside of her walls. It only took several strokes of Nicole's hand to hit the G-spot.

"Umm fuck me Nicky I'm about to give it to you, please don't move," Jamie spoke in ecstasy as she gyrated her hips to meet Nicole's hand. "Harder baby, fuck me harder. Ooooh shit." Jamie's body jerked uncontrollably as she held onto Nicole's neck. While slipping in and out of consciousness she realized that someone was standing by watching them.

Chapter 19

Destiny walked discreetly up the steps. Not wanting to bring any attention to herself, she had decided not to use the overhead lighting to guide her through the dimness that now engulfed the attic. Taking her steps one at a time she rushed over to where the Sergeant laid quietly on the ground. Destiny's observations of the area lead her to believe that Déjà had her hand in making the officer as comfortable as possible.

Destiny made a full inspection of the attic. After several minutes of looking at the Sergeant she realized that something was wrong with him. Standing directly above him, she now noticed that the Sergeant had not moved. She lowered herself at the knees and placed her head across his chest. That's when it hit her like a ton of bricks - the Sergeant was not breathing. His body felt clammy and cold. Thoughts of how they were going to get him out of there came to mind.

Renee and Shaun stood standing outside in the hallway. Destiny had told them to play chicky (look-out) while she ran upstairs. All of their belongings were packed and they were ready to go. The only thing stopping them from leaving sooner was the body that they now would have to carry with them. While waiting around nervously, Renee tip-toed down the hall, peeked her head around the corner and saw that the stairwell was clear; all the bedrooms were empty and fortunately for them the sun was going down. Renee couldn't wait to get on the road back to New York City.

Butterflies was giving her a real eerie feeling. Tip- toeing back to where Shaun stood by the attic door, she told her that everything was clear. "I think everyone is downstairs setting up for the party." "Yeah, I know". Shaun whispered. "I saw Jamie and Nicole heading downstairs earlier." "I don't know Jamie, Destiny is taking long maybe we should go upstairs and check on her." "Nah, she told us to stay here." "I didn't hear you say anything about her," Shaun asked as she pointed towards Angie's room. "Where is Angie," Renee questioned looking over her shoulder. "I don't know," Shaun replied. "I haven't seen her since the accident." "She's probably downstairs with the others," Renee responded as an afterthought. "Don't you find the house a bit too quiet? I mean isn't there suppose to be a party getting ready to take place. This house is getting creepier by the minute." Shaun wrapped her arms around herself. "Shut up Shaun. You sound like you're scared. We wouldn't be in this mess if your ass wouldn't have panicked," Renee was hyped up. She had a good mind of walking back into her bedroom grabbing her Louis Vuitton overnight bag and leaving without Destiny.

Her mind went into overdrive when she thought about the consequence of helping Shaun. Destiny's plan wasn't full proof because it wasn't guaranteed that they could pull it off. Her guess was as good as any, besides why should she jeopardize her future for someone else? Yeah, she owed Destiny for the time she had come to her rescue that night on 8th Avenue, but she didn't owe Shaun shit. "Who the fuck is you to tell me to shut up Ne!" "You bitch!" "I got your bitch!" Shaun stepped back

134

placing herself in a fighting position with her hands balled up into fists. Shaun was ready for anything Renee brought her way. She was tired, afraid and aggravated and she wasn't about to let Renee disrespect her.

Unnoticed Angie came around the corner. "Whatever Shaun, it ain't like you in any position to do anything. That's why your ass is in trouble now. You act like a mutherfucker owe you something." "What the hell are you talking about? I didn't ask you to do shit for me. Destiny is the one who offered to help me out." "Stop whining," Renee stated dismissing Shaun with a wave of her hand.

"Don't be trying to dismiss me Ne!" Shaun jumped in her face. Before they were able to continue with their brawl, Angie stepped in between them. "Hey what the fuck are you two fighting about?" Shaun and Renee looked at each other as if to say "Oh shit." In a moment of anger they had lost the focus.

Destiny had been walking down the steps in hopes of putting a stop to Renee's arguing. When Destiny was about to exit the attic she overheard Angie, and with her hand on the doorknob, she held back. She stood with her back firmly against a wall, and then continued to listen to the voices that were coming from the other side.
"Why aren't you guys getting ready for the party?" Angie released the belt that held her robe together, show boating her costume while making a full circle so the other ladies could take a look. "Damn girl. That costume is off the hook," Shaun complimented. "Yeah, I know its different right?" "What's so

135

different about it Angie? I've seen that get up a hundred times before," Renee butted in. "Renee you are so determined to knock a bitch down when their at their best, that you don't even realize that your only making yourself look like a fool." Angie twirled around giving Renee her ass to kiss. "Angie where are you going," Shaun questioned awkwardly. "To finish getting dressed, you should do the same if you don't want Ma'dam Déjà to get on you for being late," glaring in Renee's direction Angie uttered sorely.

"You should have started hours ago Renee. You know it takes you a long time to master what only takes others a few minutes." Walking off without giving them a second thought Angie laughed. "That bitch, I should run up in her piece and bash her fuckin head in." "I wouldn't do that if I were you," Destiny stated as she stepped out into the hallway. "I'm so glad your ass decided to join us." "Listen girl I ain't got time for your shit, we have real problems." Destiny was talking quickly all along searching the hallways for unwanted company." "We, there ain't no we. My ass is out of here either your going with me or not Des." Shaun watched on as the best friends went back and forth."O.k. o.k. let me think." "Think, ain't nothing to think about. This is not our problem Des we came here for one reason and one reason only. Everything else is irrelevant!" Grabbing Destiny by the shoulders, Renee looked deeply into her eyes. "Stop trying to play save-a-hoe. We have to get out of here." "Renee the Sergeant is dead!" "What! How? When," Shaun gasped. "When I went upstairs to check on him he wasn't breathing." Sadly Renee could see the worry in Destiny's eyes.

"What the hell are you talking about," Renee asked while making a mad dash up the stairs. Once she reached the top landing, Renee walked swiftly toward Sergeant Wilcox, placing her hand at the side of his neck. She searched for a pulse ... there wasn't one, realizing that Destiny was not over reacting Renee burst into tears. "This is crazy," she said between sobs. Shaun who was standing right behind her, felt like her whole world had just come to a complete stop.

Trying desperately to gain her composure, Shaun placed her freshly manicured hand on Renee's shoulder. Sergeant Wilcox's body was already cold and in a few hours rigor mortis would begin you set in. Running at this point would only show guilt where there was none. Renee couldn't believe how life, with its twist and turns, had dealt her such a raw hand. Now there was no way that she could leave Ma'dam Déjà or Butterflies for that manner, unless of course she had come up with a plan to benefit herself.

Suddenly a light bulb went off in her head. She stood up, wiped away the tears that streamed from her eyes, and then she turned around with a blank stare. "Shaun go out the shed and get me the chainsaw." "What are you going to do Nene," Shaun questioned her, afraid that Renee had lost her mind. "Don't ask me no fucking questions, just do it!" Renee slowly turned back towards the corpse. "Misdeal mutherfucka," Renee whispered.

She refused to go back to prison, making the body disappear would be the best thing they could do.

Chapter 20

Nadiva and Brianna giggled at their mother's voice. After swinging an episode with Nick, Déjà headed over to her cottage to bathe, eat a light dinner and spend some time with her daughters. Cat in the hat by Dr. Seuss had turned out to be a big hit in her household. Déjà's little ladies really enjoyed the story, the pictures and the added bonus, spending time with their mom.

When spending quality time with her daughters, Déjà was able to get in touch with her inner child. She became playful and full of animation, bringing the characters in the book to life, causing her daughters to scream out in laughter. Butterflies, was taking a lot of time away from them. And now, as she sat close and cozy with them, Déjà realized that she was missing out on the simple things in life. Nadiva was growing up fast. Brianna had lost her first tooth and she wasn't there to play tooth fairy, something every child should experience. Being a mother was totally different from being a parent. Anyone could give birth to a child, but it was the parenting aspect that mattered, the nurturing, teaching and guiding that made your creation blossom.

Being able to be there for her daughters was very important to Déjà. They were gifts given to her by GOD, and gifts such as these could not be taken for granted. Déjà's dream of living a life free of worries was slowly becoming just that a dream. She could remember a frame with a special saying hanging in Mrs.

Negron's office which read, "Obstacles are the things you see when you take your eyes off your goals." Clearly Déjà could see the slogan for what it was. Mrs. Negron had it laminated and hung in her office when Déjà had first arrived at Our Lady of Hope. Those fourteen little words had become the force that helped Déjà overcome her fear of being a single parent. Making it on her own had become her main priority. Through lots of therapy Déjà was determined to give her daughters a better life.

As she thought about that now, she wasn't sure that she had made the right choices. What had she been thinking when she came up with this crazy scheme of opening up a whorehouse? Selling coochie was not the type of profession a woman would choose if she had the responsibilities that she did. Déjà had two little people who depended on her. What would happen to them if she wasn't around to raise them? Surely Children's Services would get involved. Déjà couldn't imagine her daughters living a life of emptiness, while their mother sat in a prison cell, longing for them.

Her eyes became misty as those thoughts filled her mind. Nick promised her that she would take care of the dilemma she now faced … hopefully she will. In all reality every single one of her ladies could walk away right now and Déjà would be left holding the bag. She tried not to think about something like that happening, so she snuggled closer to her girls, longing to feel their comfort. All she wanted to do was to enjoy them.

The moment of truth had come though, and Déjà had to get ready for whatever came her way. Placing one of the many masks she learned to create throughout her life of hardship, bringing the book to an end, Déjà called her Russian nanny over and instructed her to get the girls ready for bed. She kissed them both goodnight, then headed towards the bedroom to get ready.

Jheri leaned up against the wall when her eyes connected with Jamie's. She had walked in on something she knew she was not suppose to witness. Surprised that Nicole and Jamie would expose their lust for one another so openly, Jheri had decided to stick around for the show. Jheri always fantasized about two feminine women getting their freak, on as she laid in the cut watching. Its funny how when you least expect it, your fantasy would come true.

Walking in on Jamie when she was about to release her orgasm had been a real treat for her. Jheri had a good mind to just walk in, sit down on one of the sofas and make her presence fully known. However she didn't want to interrupt their flow. So she just stood by the entryway. Her cover was blown though, so she tried to disappear by placing her back against a wall, but it was too late. She could hear the ladies whispering in the background as they moved around the room adjusting their clothes.

Then Jheri heard footsteps coming in her direction. When the ladies came into view, Jheri tried to press her back closer to the wall. Nicole who was the more daring of the two, placed her face to Jheri's and kissed her on the lips. Pulling back some, Nicole sensed that Jheri was getting turned on. Reaching into her pants Jheri's pussy had become wet. "Ummm girl you sure as hell know how to bring a nigga to her knees," Jheri stated as she grabbed Nicole's hand and pressed it deeper into her. "Baby you haven't seen anything yet." "Oh yeah." "Yeah." Kissing Jheri once more, Nicole asked her, "Can you taste her Jay? She tastes real sweet doesn't she?" "You are a freaky little something ain't you," Jamie asked Nicole as she walked out of the living room and into the hallway. "I can't believe your continuing the party without me." "Come here girl," Jheri pulled Jamie close to her. Jheri and Nicole devoured each other's mouths while Jheri reached under Jamie's skirt and played with her.

Eric Miller couldn't believe how freely Nicole jumped from one sex scene to the next. His image of her had been shattered. Thankfully, his gut feeling caused him to return back to Butterflies to witness the freak show. C.O. Miller turned away from the window disappointed and he disappeared back into the woods. While he walked along the path, something continued to nag at him. He couldn't quite put his finger on it. Nevertheless his instincts never failed him before. Although Nicole's freak show captured his attention he still remained focused on the situation at hand - Sergeant Wilcox was still nowhere to be found and if Eric didn't do something about it, he wouldn't be able to live with himself. Coming across the number he searched for on his cell phone, Eric pressed speed dial. After several rings, Eric urgently asked the receptionist to connect him with the Inspector General's Unit.

Chapter 21

To say that Déjà looked gorgeous was an understatement. As she sashayed through the front door of her establishment, everyone gathered around in admiration. Dressed like Elvira the princess of darkness, Déjà strutted into the living room where the gentlemen who had arrived for the masquerade party stood around in casual conversation while drinking cocktails. The guest weren't the only ones that looked on in amazement; Madam Déjà gazed at her guest too. All dressed in some mysterious type of costume along with masks to disguise their true identity. She was pleased to find that the party was in full swing.

Her ladies had done a great job of decorating. Candles flickered against dark walls as there shadows danced. The lights had been turned down low giving the room a strange and frightening appearance. Before the guests arrived for the evening, champagne glasses were set on silver platters that were now to be passed around by two young ladies, who also wore mask. Déjà assumed they were from the catering service she had hired to prepare exotic dishes and serve drinks.

On the invitations, Déjà had made it a point to ask everyone who attended to wear the color black. The party was to bring a mystical aura that was meant to bring an evening of adventure and mystery. So far that's exactly how the gathering was turning out to be. Making several rounds, Déjà acknowledged each guest by nodding her head, recognizing them immediately, not by their face but by the outline of their physique. They could have paper bags over their heads and she would still know who was who. How could she not recognize them? She had slept with half of the gentlemen who now filled her home with their superior attitudes. Underneath, her smile Déjà held a sinister grin. She couldn't imagine how these men who's reputations in law enforcement was held at such high levels, if ever placed under investigation they would be stripped of their superficial bullshit, exposed for who they really were. Freaks! Their weakness for pussy had become Déjà's key to turning her pass situations around to benefit her.

Déjà pulled out her little black book filled with her customers' names and personal numbers, while dressing in her cottage. Some of the most prestigious men in Corrections were in this book. Who would dare to come after her on a murder charge, with all of the information she held in the palm of her hand. Confident that she could use this information to her advantage, Déjà crossed the manicured lawns toward the main house with one agenda and one agenda only.

While reaching for a glass of champagne, Déjà stopped midway when she felt the waitress giving her direct eye contact. There was something about how she glared at her that made her feel uneasy. It was too direct and out of the norm for hired help to behave in such a disrespectful manner. Finally coming in full contact with the stem of the champagne glass, Déjà asked for her name. "My name is Star." "Well Star, has anyone ever told you that it is rude to stare at people," Déjà

146

snapped back while placing the rim of the glass to her lips. She took a sip of the cold substance and then continued, "Especially the host!" "Excuse me ma'dam those were not my intentions, it's just that your costume," Star, whose real name happened to be investigator Rochelle Leach, from the Inspector General's Office said while looking at Déjà up and down. "It's umm how would I say, so provocative." "Well thank you Star. Would it be safe to say that my costume is maybe even challenging," Déjà's stated as she glided her index finger in between her breast.

Her sixth sense kicked in. Déjà could tell by the way that she looked at her that this Star character was not your regular hired help. Walking off to mingle with her guests, Déjà detected that there were one, maybe two individuals at the party who were not invited, but there to create static.

Déjà observed one of her most loyal and devoted customers standing by the bar nursing what seemed to be a glass of whiskey. Mr. Dunn had received his invitation personally from her. Although their sessions together were becoming too few and far between, Déjà always tried to show her gratitude, by accepting his calls immediately without any delay. His friendship toward Déjà had always been one of pure sincerity. Even after her time as a call girl had become a demand among other men, she never neglected to handle her business when it came to him.

Together they had instituted a way where Mr. Dunn wouldn't be exposed to Déjà's place, yet he received and benefited from

147

what Déjà had to offer. Her house call visits to him had become much more than just a roll in the hay, Mr. Dunn had become her confidant; he was a good listener and Déjà found that she could speak with him about anything. His opinions mattered too. Suddenly she could recall that at their last meeting Mr. Dunn had expressed some concerns.

Albion N.Y. was such a small town, so Mr. Dun occasionally ran into the people who were connected to the Correctional Facility. New Orleans was quickly being introduced to ma'dam Butterflies Establishment as well. At Tops, a local supermarket chain, Dunn had overheard a conversation between two ladies who were standing by the produce department who were adamant about finding out exactly what was going on at Butterflies. Their husbands had begun to come home at all hours of the night, calling at first claiming that they had to work overtime or had to escort someone in inmate population on a medical trip. These ladies never had a reason to not trust their husbands, but once the gentlemen arrived home at 2, 3, 4 o'clock in the morning, doubts began to settle in of course. The smell of perfume on their person didn't help much with arousing their suspicions.

"Listen, Déjà, I realize that you have put a lot of work into your business, but I am a little concerned," Mike began to say as he zipped up his pants while moving in on Déjà, so that she could fully understand the seriousness of his next words. "The people in this town are starting to talk." "Yeah what are they saying Mike," Déjà asked as she reached into her Gucci bag to get her

148

lip gloss. "The wives of all these men who indulge in your girls are beginning to form an investigation against Butterflies." "Oh yeah well I have nothing to worry about Mike. You know that I'm protected and besides do you really believe that my clients will allow themselves to get caught up in some type of scandalous rumor. Because that's what it is, a rumor."

"Déjà please don't fool yourself into believing that these women wouldn't go the extra mile to expose you. The men are not going to protect you, they are only going to look out for themselves." Mike who enjoyed Déjà's company on a sexual level had also taken a liking to her on a personal one. He would hate to see her get caught up in something she couldn't get herself out of. He felt that she had already been through enough in life and deserved so much more.

"I think that you should shut Butterflies down. You've had a good six months, and you should have enough money now to move onto something much more productive, like real estate." "I'm a C.O. Mike. Did you forget that I already have a career," Déjà questioned with a wicked smile. "No I didn't, smarty pants. Look I'm just trying to look out for you." "I know Mike and honestly I appreciate it. But don't worry about me I have everything under control." "I hope so Déjà." Déjà turned her back to him, reached into her bag again then pulled out a small white envelope. "Here!" "What is this?" "It's an invitation to my masquerade party." "Masquerade party," Mike asked with a question mark dancing in his eye. "Yes masquerade. That means costumes, masks, drinks, dancing, dinner and desert,"

Déjà giggled. "Desert ummm!" "Don't be late Mike I'll be expecting you. You really need to get out more often." Walking away Déjà looked over her shoulder and said. "Mike." "Yeah?" "Thanks for everything." "Your very welcomed, pretty lady."

Déjà quickly left Mike's house, jumped in her truck and headed toward Albion's C.F. Her shift was about to begin and she didn't want to be late. Thinking back at how Mike was trying to warn her she had decided she wasn't ready to deal with him just yet. She did smile in his direction though. Then once again she made eye contact with Star.

Chapter 22

Meanwhile in the attic, Renee patiently and carefully cut Sergeant Wilcox's limbs. After sawing off his right leg and getting over the initial shock of what she was doing, removing all if his other body parts were simple. Destiny stood besides, her collecting each body piece as they came undone, while Shaun held a black hefty bag open. The act turned out to be a team effort, like everything else they had planned to do.

The realization of what they were committing hadn't quite hit them on a mental level. All they knew was that they, together, had made a pledge to help each other through this. They planned to get the body out of the house and into the truck, without being noticed. Then they would get rid of the body somewhere along the highway, as they traveled back to New York City. Through the sound of the electric saw, Renee could hear the music being played just one level below.

The voices coming through the vents informed her that the festivities were well on its way. It was only a matter of time before the social gathering would break into couples of two or three and head up to the second level to indulge in all kinds of sexual entertainment. Time was of the essence and time didn't stop for no one. Carefully they wrapped things up making sure that all the evidence was destroyed. They quickly changed their clothes, throwing them in the bag along with the Sergeant, replacing their costumes, garter belts, sheer stockings, and satin panties with something much more appropriate for the task like jeans, hoodies and Timbs. The ghetto wear they had chosen was just a reminder of where they had come from. Butterflies and Déjà was just a front, a façade of who they really were. Thug-ettes to the heart, do or die bitches with no time to spare. It was all or nothing when it came to their hood mentality. They each grabbed a bag then headed down the steps.

Jheri had been on the second level of the house for quite some time. She was double checking the rooms for suitability. Jheri placed condoms, dental dam, exotic oils and other little treats Déjà's clients used for their enjoyment. Coming upon the attic, Jheri placed her ear against the door, where she heard footsteps descending. She was not aware that there was anyone else throughout the house. All of the ladies were suppose to be downstairs. To her surprise the door opened slowly and Renee's head peaked out. Coming face to face with Jheri, Renee placed her index finger up to her lips, instructing her to be quiet. One by one Renee, Destiny and Shaun exited the attic, carrying the black hefty bags securely in their hands.

Pale and sweaty from their work, Jheri realized that these young women were not the same women Déjà had groomed them to be. Not even in the P-Nile did Jheri see this side of them. Their attire was strictly street wear. Their attitude ghetto-fied, but most importantly it was their eyes - they were hollow. Before Jheri jumped to conclusions, she decided that it was best for her to just ask them what the hell they were up to. "Yo Nene what's going on?" "Ain't nothing." "It sure as hell doesn't look like nothing," Jheri stated as she glanced at the bags. "Was everything alright up there," she continued. "Yeah why," Renee responded with attitude in her voice. "I'm just asking. What's the fuckin attitude about?"

Shaun who already felt bad about putting Renee and Destiny in such a fucked up situation had stepped up. "Jheri we were just checking up on the Sergeant, but everything is cool." "Oh yeah, then what's in the bags?" "Oh these are some things we found upstairs, we are going to use them as props for the party," Destiny said as she tossed the bag she was holding over her shoulder. "Use for what," Jheri continued to ask refusing to let up.

"Come on Jheri why don't you stop with the 50 questions," Renee snapped. She was not in the mood to deal with Jheri. "Jheri you know we don't have time for your bullshit." Renee walked away as fast as possible. As a last minute thought, Shaun turned back towards Jheri, in hopes of getting some type of sympathy from her. She noticed Jheri standing motionless at the end of the hall. She was staring down at the cream colored carpet that now turned a shade of brown.

Seeing what Jheri was seeing, Shaun became paralyzed at the sight of blood that trailed behind her. "Renee!" "What Shaun? Come on," Renee responded without looking back. Destiny turned around instead; she was about to scream on Shaun for holding up the process, but then thought twice about it when she too noticed the blood stains. At that point Destiny knew

153

they were done off, pulling Shaun by the arm, Destiny told her to move and to move fast. "We got to get the hell out of here!"

Standing in front of a full length mirror, Nick admired her reflection, wearing a black Armani two piece suit, Roberto Cavalli ankle high leather boots, and black ribbed wife beater as an added touch. She estimated her timing by the sound of the voices vibrating through the floor panel. Once the festivities broke off and the passage ways to the backyard were cleared, Nick would go to work. Getting Sergeant Wilcox out of the house should be a challenge. However most of the guests would be too busy getting their freak on to notice anything else, but the pussy that would be in their faces.

Putting on the final touches to her disguise, Nick walked over to her nightstand, pulled the drawer out and reached for a small Tiffany jewelry box. As she flipped the top opened, Nick's eyes sparkled against the diamonds that sat firmly joined to a solid gold wedding band. Déjà had no idea about what was planned, but tonight after the all of the guests were gone, Nick had every intention on proposing to her. Since gay marriages were now permissible in other states, she wanted to make that move.

Nick was fully aware that Déjà's plans of becoming the best known Ma'dam in the United States was coming to an end. Nick wanted nothing more than to show her that there was more to life then the sex industry. Accepting Déjà's lifestyle, she realized she was madly in love with her and it was not easy, however, it was thought out. She loved her more than anything. And anyone who tried to interfere would be placed on

154

her shit list. Her determination to go through with her business venture left no room for anything else. Nick was not about to give into Déjà's weakness. There was a beast inside of her that was detrimental even to herself when unleashed. Placing the mask over her eyes and before stepping out into the hallway, Nick took one last look at her in the mirror and winked.

Chapter 23

Gliding through the living room, Déjà came to stand by the fireplace, observing her surroundings with caution. Star, the waitress, was becoming too comfortable with her conversations. Making small talk with Déjà's clients was not part of her job description, Déjà thought to herself as she watched her. Unaware that Déjà was keeping a close eye on her, Star walked around the room working the clients with her friendly demeanor, familiarizing herself with the guest. She took mental pictures of everyone Déjà had invited, and Déjà was taking mental pictures of her. Star made herself look so obvious it was easy for Déjà to catch on; Déjà sensed that there was more to Star than meets the eye. Her gut instinct screamed loud enough for her to listen.

Kelly Leak, an African American female, who had begun her career in Corrections by working the long hours as a C.O. had finally arrived. Advancing her way through the ranks in the department, Kelly had decided that after years of dedication to D.O.C and the many roles she played, she would eventually transfer into the Inspector General Unit. When the opportunity arose earlier in the year, she personally headed to Albany to hand deliver her resume. Submitting herself completely to her position, Kelly trained nonstop in investigations and research.

Going undercover was something she wanted more than anything. When first approached by her superiors concerning C.O. Déjà Padilla's dual personality, Kelly Leak agreed that she would be the perfect one for the job. Being that she too was versatile, Kelly discovered that after hours of researching the Ma'dam C.O.'s file she was a bonafide competitor. It took a lot of heart on Déjà's part to play out the two roles. Although it was wrong, Kelly could see how easy it would be to lure female inmates towards Butterflies; so she admired Déjà's will to make it happen.

Déjà must have outlined her plan with extreme measures when she created her business because the attraction to that type of lifestyle was not farfetched among the young ladies she had made her own. These women, Kelly discovered as she moved on into their files, were young, adventurous and electrifyingly beautiful. They only lacked one important element, self-esteem. It doesn't matter how beautiful a woman can be, if their self-esteem is low, they are two dollars short of buying into anything; feeding on negative messages and thoughts, resulting with neglecting themselves of anything that spelled success. Déjà was clever in her hunt, by focusing on the weak because they thought that they were worthless.

Kelly liked her style she too had come from the streets of Harlem N.Y., however she wasn't on the same road. Kelly had crossed over to the other side all before the streets could swallow her whole. Standing close by, dressed in a black and white tuxedo suit, Kelly submitted to her attraction towards Déjà. It was no wonder the men were drawn to Butterflies because Déjà was gorgeous, sexy and 100% enticing. She wouldn't have mind crawling in between her thighs, so Kelly wondered how much Déjà charged for her services. If given the chance Kelly wouldn't mind having Déjà's legs wrapped around her shoulders as she sucked on her clit until she exploded. Maybe once this was all over she could play out her desire for a lesser price because under extreme pressure Déjà might be willing to do just about anything.

Star made her way around the room slowly. Once she reached Kelly's side, she carefully looked around the room then asked her, "Aren't you going upstairs to check out the rest of the house?" "Yeah, I'm just waiting for the right moment. Timing is everything." "We don't have much time Kelly. We have to find out what happened with Sergeant Wilcox." "Be easy Star, we'll get all the information we need. I promise you." "Okay I'm just letting you know that now would be the time. Déjà is too busy with her guests to notice you. But you do what you have to do." Star walked away. Her best bet was to allow Kelly to do her thing without any further interruptions. Kelly knew what she was doing, at least she hoped.

Meanwhile Destiny, Renee and Shaun creped down the back steps, only a few feet away. Quietly making it to the first floor, they walked across the kitchen, and then disappeared into the night. Looking back from time to time, Destiny, the leader of the three, waved them on. Once they reached Shaun's Land Rover, they jumped in, disposing the bags with Sergeant Wilcox's body parts in the back compartment. Reaching into their luggage they pulled out clean clothing, changing quickly before driving down the road.

Nick and Déjà moved quickly from opposite directions towards the attic. "You ready," Nick questioned Déjà, who stood before her with sweat forming on her forehead. "Yeah, let's do this." Together they walked up the steps. Staying close behind Nick, Déjà kept her head down looking at the floor, taking her time with each step; hoping not lose her balance and land on her ass. That's when Déjà noticed the red stains that now began to set in, pulling at Nick's arms Déjà tried to tell her about it, however the words wouldn't come out she had no voice. "Stop pulling me Déjà. What the fuck wrong with you?" Déjà remained silent. "Yo I'm talking to you." Before Nick was able to turn around and face her. She too had noticed the blood. "Oh shit what the fuck!"

Nick ran up the steps, leaving Déjà to stand alone. Upon reaching her destination, Nick lowered herself to where Sergeant Wilcox was supposed to be. She ran her fingers through the stained blankets, then brought them up to her nose. It smelled like blood, it looked like blood so it had to be blood. Nick thoughts raced as she tried to figure out what the hell was going on. She looked over her shoulder to find Déjà looking dumbfounded. "What's going on baby," Déjà asked. "I have no idea. All I know is that the shit is about to hit the fan." "It's worse than that Nick." "Yeah I know." "Where is Shaun?" "I don't know, I haven't seen her in a minute." "Well don't you think you should look for her," Déjà hollered "Why the fuck are you getting nasty with me," Nick asked "Fuck that, I'll do it myself," Déjà stated as she turned around and left Nick bent over a puddle of blood.

In her mind she played several scenarios, and the one that stuck out the most, the one that she refused to believe, was that Shaun killed the sergeant and moved the body to another location.

Chapter 24

In the heat of the moment, Déjà completely forgot that she had a party going on downstairs. She stormed through the second level of the house, entering each room without so much as knocking on the door. Déjà inspected the bedrooms hoping to come across something that would indicate what happened to Wilcox.

As she entered Shaun's room, she noticed the closet door slightly opened. She walked over to it and found that it was empty of all its contents. Shaun must have packed her bags and left. Déjà thought that Shaun had become too frightened to deal with what she had done and had decided to leave. She stormed out of Shaun's room and into Renee's. There she found the same thing, empty closets and the dresser drawers tussled.

Before she could even consider going into Destiny's room, she already knew what she would find because Renee and Destiny were a packaged deal, if one was to leave the other would follow. The question was where did they go? And what did they do with Sergeant Wilcox? Were they bold enough to kill him and then take the evidence with them? And in who's car? Déjà couldn't come up with one single answer. Things at Butterflies were getting real ugly. All fingers would be pointing at her and she wouldn't be able to handle that. On a hunch, she decided to go to Destiny's bedroom anyway.

Standing in the middle of Destiny's bedroom Déjà noticed some torn up pieces of stationary over by the nightstand, so she quickly walked over and grabbed them. Piecing them back together like a jigsaw puzzle, Déjà was able to retrieve an address and telephone number in New York City.

Nick waited by the threshold, sensing that Déjà was on to something. The mystery of where the girls were would soon be revealed. On the same token, Déjà felt Nick close by because their connection was strong like that. Déjà turned around on her heels and ran towards her, yelling. "Baby they're on their way back to the city!" "Where?" "Some place in Harlem." "What do you want to do Déjà?" Déjà didn't have a clue as to what to do next. She looked at Nick directly, knowing that she had to do something quickly. If not, she could kiss her daughters good-bye. That thought alone should have given her the strength to make her move, nevertheless there were many things holding her back. The main thing was what she would find, once she arrived at the address she had already filed in her memory bank.

Rolling up in Harlem, and making claims wouldn't be a smart move. She really didn't have much of a choice though - it was either that or taking her chances with some of Albion's finest. While seriously considering what her options were Déjà's eyes cleared up. Nick, on the other hand, had a few ideas in mind as to what they could do, however she wasn't about to make any suggestions. Déjà was her own woman, and knowing her the way that she did, Déjà was capable of coming up with a solid solution. So Nick waited patiently for her woman to reach a decision. Whatever she choose to do, Nick was riding it out with her. It was only a matter of planning things out carefully.

Meanwhile, Jamie and Angie casually strutted around the living room smiling and flirting; playfully having conversations regarding the party, their costumes and what choice of deserts their guests should taste first. Star also conversed with the guests, but her conversation was based on the sex industry. She carefully and discreetly asked questions regarding Butterflies, such as how long had the girls been working here? How long has the gentlemen been coming to the house? These questions were so common amongst the guests that no one was suspicious of her inquiry. Most of the guests were so caught up in Jamie and Angie's asses that they didn't notice anything else.

Kelly thought it was the perfect time to creep upstairs to do some snooping around. From the reports she had read, she knew that there were six prostitutes working at Butterflies and two she/he's who played the part of security. Déjà had been the target of her investigation; however if she could get the other girls to cooperate, nailing Déjà would be easy. For several minutes she mingled amongst the guests, in hopes of getting some information about the girls.

Kelly found it strange that out of the six women only two were working the room, while Déjà, Nick, Jheri, Shaun, Renee and Destiny had been missing in action for quite some time. Something just didn't sit right with Kelly; there was definitely going on. Her sixth sense told her that the answers to what she was seeking were on the second level of the house, so Kelly proceeded to climb the stairs.

On the second floor, Kelly felt as though she had just walked into a dungeon. All of the lights were turned down low and there were cobb webs covering the walls and ceiling. Without the few candles that sat on old fashioned candle holders, Kelly wouldn't have been able to see anything around her. Opening her blazer, she placed her hand on the 9mm Glock she carried on her waistband. She hoped that she wouldn't need to use it, but one couldn't believe that it was not possible. Slowly walking up the hallway, she came up to the first bedroom. She peeked her head in and found that it was elegantly decorated, but it was empty. She continued on to the second room, which was also designed to suit its purpose, but like the first it too was empty. However, room three was not.

Kelly heard voices coming from behind the closed door. She recognized the feminine voice as being Déjà, but couldn't recognize the masculine voice. The one thing Kelly knew for sure was that it didn't belong to a man; that voice belonged to another woman. In the reports it was noted that Nick, Déjà's lover and body guard, was none other than Nakia Jackson, an ex-offender who had been recently released from Albion Correctional Facility. It was also noted that the six women who worked at Butterflies, were also ex-offenders. What Kelly couldn't quite put together was how Déjà received government funding to open up a halfway house in this name, and then use

166

it as a whorehouse. Kelly also was able to figure out how she got away with this scheme for so long. But as far as she was concerned, Déjà and her home was officially closed.

Chapter 25

Déjà spoke softly when she had finally decided which route to take on the situation. The journey was not going to be an easy one, but it sure was the one she was willing to take in order to clear her name. "Nick I've decided to follow these crazy ass bitches to New York." "Then what, Déjà?" "What do you mean, then what?" "Yeah, then what?" "Look Nick I have to find out what they did with Sergeant Wilcox. For all I know they killed him then buried the body. That alone will send me to prison for 25 years. Is that what you want?"

Déjà grabbed Nick by the hand and held her stare. "Of course not. You know I love the shit out of you." "Okay then let me do what I need to do," Déjà stated then asked as an afterthought. "Are you going with me?" "I don't know, should I? " "Yes of course you should. I need you." "And why is that? Why should I sacrifice my freedom for you?" "Because I love you and I promise that nothing will go wrong. We'll just go down there, talk to the girls and find out where the Sergeant is, then bounce." "Bounce huh. I love it when you get gangster." "Oh yeah!" "Yeah, Come over here and give me a kiss."

Nick grabbed Déjà and kissed her gently on her lips then said, "There is only one way that I will ride this out with you." "What's that?" Nick reached into her pocket and pulled out a small ring box from Tiffany's. Déjà's eyes opened in surprised. "What is this Nick?" "It's the only way I'll go to New York City with you." "You have to be joking right?"

Not sure what Nick meant by her gesture, Déjà played it safe by taking the box out of Nick's hand. She opened the box to see a two carat diamond engagement ring tightly snuggled in velvet bedding. Déjà couldn't believe her eyes. Everything she had tried to avoid, as far as her relationship with Nick was concerned, was now staring her in the face. She couldn't possibly be serious. Déjà had no intentions of marrying a woman; in her eyes it was not ethical. Two women having an affair was one thing, but to outright go in front of an alter and commit their lives to each other was something else.

Déjà thought about her answer before she looked away from the sparkling gem. "Déjà will you marry me," Nick asked her with so much sincerity in her voice. Déjà's heart broke, for reasons Nick would eventually find out. Now was not the time to express her true outlook on gay marriages because she needed Nick to ride with her to New York. Once she settled her differences with Destiny, Renee and Shaun, she would sit Nick down and talk to her.

"Yes baby I will marry you!" "You serious Dee? You'll really do this?" "Yes I will, I love you Nick." Nick hugged Déjà, picked her up off the ground and swung her around. Nick was happier than a gay man incarcerated with 1200 men. Déjà, on the other hand, was not. Behind Nick's back Déjà screwed her face up. "Okay baby chill we have to get ready to leave." "What? You mean now?" Nick released Déjà. "Right now. We can't wait another minute." "Now you are the one who has to be joking." "Nah I'm dead ass serious." "What about all the people that are downstairs," Nick asked while pointing towards the floor. "What about them?" "Déjà you can't just walk out of here without them noticing." "Who said we are walking out the front door," Déjà smiled wickedly. "Oh you're a nasty girl," Nick smiled at the thought. "Yeah I know. Now let's go," Déjà demanded with a wink.

Kelly, who had been standing outside of the door listening in on Déjà and Nick, moved quickly down the hall. She hurriedly went back down the stairs and gave Star a signal. Star walked over to her and asked. "What's up?" "The Madam C.O. is getting ready to hit the road." "Where to?" "New York City." "Why," Star asked confused. "Because three of her girls took Sergeant Wilcox with them." "Why?" "Damn Star why the fuck are you asking me? I don't know. All I know is that in order to find him we have to follow Ms.Padilla." "Alright so let's go." "We have to wait for her to make her move." "Okay I'll be ready." Star walked away and began to serve drinks again as though nothing was happening.

Déjà and Nick's destiny was in the hands of three scandalous females who tried to change their lives. Unfortunately for them the old saying, "you can take a girl out of the hood, but you can't take the hood out of the girl," becomes very much a fact for them and not a myth.

To be continued.....

Things are not always what they seem … and in a world full of betrayal find out if Déjà makes it out of Harlem alive with all the information she needs…..In the sequel DELAYED REACTION!

DELAYED REACTION

COMING SOON

2007

Sneak Preview

DELAYED REACTION

By Sexy

Chapter 1

"Damn girl why the fuck are you driving so fast. You act like we really going to run into them on this highway..." Nick held on to the dash board as Déjà drove down I-95 at 100 miles per hour. Nick was not impressed with Déjà's driving skills, if anything she was pissed off and disappointed in her. All they needed was to get stopped by the state troopers they would really be shit out of luck.

"Déjà I'm not playing with your demented ass. Stop this motherfuckin truck before you make me do something crazy!"

"Like what Nick," Déjà asked as sweat ran down the side of her face. "What you going to jump out or something? Stop with the bullshit Nick. I am not going to let those stinking ass bitches get away with this shit, either you're going to be down with me or not!"

Déjà had finally come to terms with the fact that once again her life was heading in another direction. Where was she was going? She hadn't a clue, all she knew was that she had to get there; and if Nick was going to get in her way then she had to get rid of her ass somewhere along the way. Nothing was going to stop her from getting her hands on Destiny. There was no doubt in her mind that Destiny was the one who convinced

175

the others to go along with this crazy scheme. Destiny had wanted to walk in Déjà's shoes for a long time, too bad that Déjà hadn't noticed it before this. It may be too late for her to save Sergeant Wilcox but she was not going to allow anyone to stand in the way of saving herself ... not even Nick.

"Déjà please baby you're not right," Nick stated trying another approach. "Why don't you pull over at the next rest stop and let me drive."

Thinking twice about what nick was saying Déjà tried to calm herself down. She was right when she called her demented because she really wasn't thinking clearly. Judging from the signs on the highway she was about to cross The George Washington Bridge into Harlem, and she remembered from all of her trips to and from the city, that there was a rest stop coming up soon.

"You're right baby. I'm sorry I'm acting all crazy," Déjà purred as she stroked Nick's face with her finger tips. "I'll pull over so we can change seats O.K."

"It's about time you've came to your senses."

"Oh come on you know you can't stay mad at me."

"And why not smart ass? That shit ain't funny." Nick pushed herself back onto the seat, and leaned her head back against the head rest. Her shoulders felt as though a ton of bricks had just been lifted off of them. "Damn this chick knows how to really stress a nigga out," Nick thought as she titled her head to the side to take a closer look at the woman she had fallen head over heels for. Déjà acted as though what Nick had to say did not matter; to look at her now, a nigga would get the impression that Déjà had a heart of stone. Never in a million years did Nick fathom that Déjà would behave so reckless.

"You are one deranged lady; I would hate to be on your shit list."

"That's why you aren't going to do anything to get on it, right Nick," Déjà stated with venom in her voice.

"Yeah alright Ma'dam princess, you swear you got your Mack down. Don't make me turn this motherfucker around Déjà. I don't even know why I allowed you to talk me into this shit. It's not like we know where the fuck we're going. Damn, I'm not even from down here and your ass knows it," Nick yelled

"You may not be from Harlem, but I am and trust me time is of the essence. We need to get to the city as quickly as possible. I don't have time to deal with your immature tantrums Nick."

Déjà spotted the rest stop sign up ahead, so she reached over the wheel to put her blinkers on. Moving her ride over to the left lane, Déjà peeked over at Nick. It was only a matter of time before she was going to find out where Destiny and the other ladies had gone. If nothing else during her initial interview with them, she had made it her business to get has much information could out of them as she possibly could. Finding

177

them shouldn't be a problem, as long as she didn't have any interference from anyone. When desperate, criminals usually go back to their old stumping grounds, hoping to find support amongst their people. Little did they know that these were the same people that were going to give Déjà all the information she needed to find them.

Coming to a complete stop, Déjà placed the gear in park then turned her body fully. Now looking directly at Nick, Déjà thinks about what she is going to say next.

"Baby I am going to the restroom it will only take a minute. Please don't be upset with me, you know I am under a lot of stress. I love you." Déjà leans forward to nibble on Nick's cheek before she grabs her bag and then opens the door.

"Yeah I know you love me, but your ass is buggin," Nick replied before Déjà was able to shut the door behind her.

"Yeah I know you love me," Déjà mimicked under her breath. Yes she had feelings for the dyke, but it was not that serious. If she had to choose between Nick and her freedom, Nick would lose the battle instantly. What fool would actually get out of an abusive relationship, then turn around and scarifies their lives for someone else? There was no way Déjà was putting anyone or anything before her own happiness. The only ones who could get that privilege were her seeds, which she now thought of as she reached the bathroom door, "God please help me find Sergeant Wilcox before it's too late. I need to get back to my girls," Déjà whispered into the air.

Slowly Déjà turned the knob, before entering the odor filled room. It wasn't one of the cleanest bathrooms Déjà had ever used, but it would just have to do for now. She needed time to think without any interruptions from Nick. Locking the door securely behind her Déjà placed her Gucci handbag on the sink then looked into the mirror. There was no wonder why Nick was spazzing out on her; her hair was a mess and standing up at attention in areas she never even knew she had hair, her black mascara ran down her face from the tears she had shed back at the house, and her clothes were hanging lose over her body. Déjà was finally coming down from the rush of all the excitement and she began to feel tired and all she wanted at this point was some sleep. Nevertheless, that was out of the question because there wasn't any time for all that drama. Déjà turned on the faucet, and when it reached the right temperature, she began to wash the stress away. After reapplying her makeup and tying her hair in a ponytail, Déjà looked flawless; her skin tone went back to normal which brought out the beauty she truly possessed. You'd be surprised what a little soap and water could do. These were some of the little things people took for granted, but not Déjà she thrived on taking care of herself. First impressions meant a lot, especially in the hood. If she was going into the slums of New York City, she had to make sure these people would be willing to talk to her. Happy with the results of her makeover Déjà casually walked out of the restroom. As she walked back over to the truck, Déjà noticed Nick over by the pay phone.

"What the hell is she doing over there? Who the fuck is she calling," Déjà questioned as paranoia began to set in. Everything inside of her, told her to jump in her truck and drive away. Trying to fight with the demons that tormented her mind, Déjà stood quietly, watching Nick from the distance. From her body language Déjà sensed that Nick was talking to another woman … But who? Was it Destiny? And if it was, why would she be talking to the enemy?

Déjà couldn't for the life of her imagine Nick being down with Destiny, but then again why not? Nick was the one who had recruited Destiny, so maybe they were in on this together? Déjà's mind was on overdrive. Deciding to deal with this at a later time she continued to walk slowly towards her truck. Being that Nick's back was turned Déjà was able to get behind the wheel unnoticed.

Looking back towards Nick, Déjà had made the conscious decision to get the hell out of there. Without hesitation and with one turn of the key, Déjà brought the Land Rover to life. Hearing the sound of a motor running behind her, Nick quickly turned towards the sound. When she noticed that it was Déjà behind the wheel, it was too late for her to do anything. Déjà, on the other hand, knew exactly what to do. This was going to be her best performance yet! She put her truck in gear and drove away, leaving Nick high and dry on I-95.

Chapter 2

"I need a girl to ride ride ride, I need a girl to be my wife, yo Renee I love that fuckin song put that shit up," Destiny called out from the back seat.

"Why don't you chill Des you act like you have been doing this type of shit every day? You need to get your ass up here and drive for a little while before I fall asleep and we end up in the Hudson River. I'm getting sleepy," Renee responded without so much as fulfilling Destiny's request.

"I already drove, its Shaun's turn, that bitch ain't been doing nothing but sleeping."

"Why don't you watch your mouth Des?"

"Watch my mouth you got to be joking." Destiny's laugh echoed over the sound that escaped the speakers. "We ain't fuckin with that Ma'dam no more, besides it's the truth … Shaun hasn't done shit but sleep the whole fuckin ride down here." Destiny suddenly turned bitter at the thought of Shaun taking the situation so lightly, and Renee's comment was not putting her in the best of moods. From her point of view it was Shaun who should have been driving in the first place. They already played their positions, now the rest was up to Miss want to knock- a - nigga out and leave- him- for -dead. And to add insult to injury she was being told how to speak again.

"Wake her sorry ass up Nene."

"Why? Leave her alone Destiny you know all she going to do is start crying all over again."

"Alright then stop complaining and put the fuckin music up, and don't be telling me to watch my mouth either. I had enough of that shit I'm not living up to somebody else's standards. As of today Destiny is going to say and do whatever the fuck she wants." With that said, Destiny looked out of the window, trying her best to ignore her agitation towards returning back to Harlem. Destiny began to sing along with the music again in hopes of forgetting the past. It had been years since her last visit to New York City and now that she was coming face to face with her past, Destiny realized that she had made a drastic choice in returning. The sight of the old tenement buildings as the car glided over The George Washington Bridge made Destiny sick with worry. That part of her life was supposed to be over. Now she wasn't sure if it was over, or if returning to the streets of Harlem was going to be just another chapter in her book of life. Either way, she was beginning to feel uncomfortable, afraid to share her thoughts with Renee; Destiny just laid her head back on her seat and closed her eyes. Visions of the block she grew up on came to mind. She could remember the many evenings she stood out at the wee hours of the morning, hanging out on 112th street and Lexington Avenue. Johnson Projects was the place to be if you were underage and couldn't get into any of the local bars. Her mother had warned her against all the shiesty characters that lingered among the pathways. But like any young girl that wanted to explore her youth, she didn't listen; learning the most important lesson of her life, that when it comes to the streets there was no loyalty amongst the living. That is why she felt the need to help Shaun. There were many times in her life that she wished someone would have scarified their lives for her. She didn't have the heart to leave Shaun out in the cold. Now that she thought about it, it must be a woman thing, although there were women out there who didn't give two shits if a sista was down and out. The new breed of women coming up nowadays would rather kick you when you're down, instead of giving you a helping hand to lift you up. Those thoughts brought Destiny to a new realization, what if those women she despised so much knew something that she didn't know. Time will soon tell if Shaun appreciated what she and Renee had done for her.

"Hey Renee."

"No Destiny I'm not putting the radio up so leave me alone."

"Nah I'm not thinking about that, I'm thinking about something else," Destiny responded with sadness in her voice.

"What is it Des? You alright back there? You sick or something?"

"No I'm not sick even though the smell is starting to get stronger."

"What smell?"

"Hellllooo Renee did you forget that we are riding around with a dead body in the trunk."

"No I didn't forget! I just didn't realize that you could smell him," Renee answered while holding the steering wheel with one hand and her nose with the other.

"Hey what is all the noise about?"

"About fuckin time Sleeping Beauty," Renee said as she looked over at Shaun.

"Damn I thought your ass was dead too," Destiny yelled out from the back seat as she turned towards the smell that was now turning her stomach.

"No I'm not dead smart ass! Did it ever occur to you, that I'm stressed out and I really can't deal with what we have done," Shaun expressed as tears began to form in the corner of her eyes.

"Oh come on I don't want to hear the shit again. You need to get a grip. You sure weren't worried about nothing when Renee drove that saw through the Sergeant's limbs."

"No I wasn't worried because I was in shock you stupid disrespectful bitch. I am so sick of you and your stupid remarks Destiny." Shaun glared into Destiny's eyes as if to say bring it.

"So, it's not like you going to do anything, Shaun, your punk ass would have still been back there tripping if it wasn't for us.

If you feel like you got the heart to deal with this on your own, give me the word and we can stop this motherfucker right now and drop you and your package off, "Destiny glared back.

There was nothing left for Shaun to say. She had no choice but to shut her mouth and deal with Destiny's wackiness. She needed Renee and Destiny to help her get rid of the body. But when that task was completed she was going to show Destiny who the punk was. That bitch needed to know that there were two sides of the coin.

Déjà Vu Publications Presents

Sexy

Order Form

Déjà vu Publications

P.O. Box 1002

New York, N.Y. 10029

Name _____

Address_____

City_____

State_____

Zip _____

Books Available:

"A Better Touch"	$ 15.00
"Twofold"	$ 15.00
"Twofold Part 2"	$ 15.00
Shipping/ Handling	$ 4.60
Total	$_____

FORMS OF ACCEPTED PAYMENTS

Institutional Checks & Money orders

Déjà Vu Publications Is now accepting Manuscripts

Write your way to success be published by the best!!!!